The Secret Adventures of Sherlock Holmes

The Secret Adventures of Sherlock Holmes
is written by Paul E. Heusinger

Published and Printed by:
Lifevest Publishing
4901 E. Dry Creek Rd., #170
Centennial, CO 80122
www.lifevestpublishing.com

Printed in the United States of America

I.S.B.N. 1-59879-153-2

The Secret Adventures of Sherlock Holmes

by Paul E. Heusinger

"Oh, a trusty comrade is always of use; and a chronicler still more so."

-Sherlock Holmes

Introduction

The short stories presented herein are original tales composed in secret by Dr. John H. Watson nearly a century ago! Sherlock Holmes, himself, explicitly forbade Watson from writing down any of the ten adventures in this collection 'until a century had gone by'.

Notwithstanding the prohibition invoked by his mentor, the ever-faithful Watson found a way to record the unrevealable chronicles while at the same time remaining in compliance with his confidant's ultimatum. Watson discovered this technique of 'psychic writing', not in a willful, rebellious, or crafty conatus; but rather in an effortless endeavor brought about by the prompting of clairvoyant forces.

The very first story reveals how Watson was able to compose the adventure in his mind, in some previously unused section of his memory, where it could be recalled in its entirety at a later date. This exercise in serendipitous learning had subsequent ramifications beyond the ken of Dr. Watson. For, the fruit of the tree of Watson's serendipity was picked a century later by myself, the presenter scribe of these secret and confidential adventures which are being presented here in print for the first time.

Sherlock Holmes and Dr. Watson encounter the gapeseed of clairvoyance in The Secret Adventure of The Vanishing Marquis, the opening story in this volume. Together, they experience and witness a demonstration of the power of a clairvoyant to overlap the physical realities of time and space. The theory of mental telepathy extant in 1906 passes over into the realm of science in the minds of our protagonists, Holmes and Watson.

In The Secret Adventure of the Psychic Connection, the second story, as the drums of war are being unpacked and brought center stage in the European theatre by a band of brainwashed teutons, comic opera princes, and nepotic kings; Sherlock Holmes is summoned to the Admiralty by the newly appointed, First Sea Lord, Sir Winston Spenser Churchill. The expansion of the German Navy has caused consternation in the English Government, according to Mycroft Holmes who has recommended his brother, Sherlock, as the one man in Britain who may be able to discern the motives of the German fleet.

July 1914 is the setting for the third story, The Secret Adventure of Irish Gunrunning. After seven hundred years England is ready to grant Home Rule to Ireland; mainly to secure her vulnerable rear in the bargain; preventing Ireland from aligning itself with Germany. The fly in the ointment of this political solution resides in the north of Ireland, in the province of Ulster, which has threatened an armed uprising, rather than become part of a self-ruling Ireland. The landing of a thousand rifles in Ulster has brought the kettle of conflict to a boil. The Prime Minister of England calls upon Sherlock Holmes to defuse the timebomb in Ireland.

The Secret Adventure of the Great White Ape, the fourth story, reveals the partial whereabouts of Sherlock Holmes during the summer of 1891; the beginning of his three year, psuedo-disappearance known as the Great Hiatus; a period during which he allegedly refrained from contacting his partner in detection, Dr. Watson. Holmes is sent for by the peerage family named Greystoke, to investigate the disappearance of family members along with the ship transporting them to British West Africa.

The Secret Adventure of the Whitechapel Murders is a documentary account of a series of brutally, viscious killings of prostitutes in London's West End during the fall of 1888. This time, the Chief Inspector of Scotland Yard, himself, sends for Holmes and implores him to find the madman who had butchered two 'unfortunates' during the month of August. Despite the combined forces of Scotland Yard and the Metropolitan Police, the City of London Police, and Sherlock Holmes and his private army known as the Baker Street Irregulars; three more innocent streetwalkers were slain in the month of September, each murder more gruesome than the last. By plotting the murder locations on a city map of London, Holmes uses Euclidean Geometry to formulate a theory predicting the next killing by the fiend who had become known as Jack-the-Ripper.

Perhaps the most shocking tale in this collection, The Secret Adventure of the Regimental Bugle Boy; this is a story of a strange and mysterious ritual in darkest Africa. Holmes receives a letter from a colonel in command of a regiment serving in British West Africa during World War I. In Nigeria, the largest of four British colonies there, the dominant Tiv tribe, slaveholding, terrorizes their helots with a bizarre, quasi-religious ceremony. Holmes takes an interest in this peculiar enigma one year later, after the end of WWI, when the bugle boy of the colonel's regiment vanishes while on leave in the British Isles.

No collection of short stories, no matter the genre, would be complete absent a Christmas tale. Dr. Watson surely shared this sentiment; with his *sui generis* retelling of the *nulli secundis*, quintessential, second-to-none, favorite memories of Christmas; as experienced by the brothers Holmes: Mycroft and Sherlock; a resplendent reminder of the noble character and the common brotherhood inherent and congenital in the family of man, despite its tendency to remain unconscious and dormant within us.

Christmas of 1918, the first in the wake of WWI, with the bells of peace enveloping Britain and the Allies, Sherlock and Mycroft invite Watson to join them at the Diogenes Club to celebrate the season of joy. After a toast to Charles Dickens, by Dr. Watson, Mycroft proposes a round of personal tale-telling based upon Dickensian themes. Sherlock agrees by appointing his brother first raconteur. Mycroft tells of their boyhood summer spent in Ireland during 1861. A summer of content: Mycroft in reading; Sherlock in exploration, seeking out the 'little people' of Irish myth and legend, and discovering the magic of Christmas in the process.

When his turn, Sherlock relates his trip to the front in December 1914 - the first of the four Christmas seasons during WWI - while on a mission for the King of England. He gives an eximious eyewitness account of the fantastic Christmas truce which befell the no man's land and opposing trenches on the eve of Christmas.

The Secret Adventure of the Banaly Woman is definitely the most revealing account concerning the personal, intimate nature of Holmes' love life I have ever recorded. Holmes insisted that any revelation of his long-term relationship with a woman - any woman - would compromise his effectiveness at solving crimes. More importantly, the personal safety of the woman in question would be jeopardized; she becoming a hostage to fortune at 221-B Baker Street.

Notwithstanding Irene Adler, the Banaly woman became the significant woman in the life of my closest friend. From their first meeting, in the British Museum, onwards; her electrifying presence was the catalyst for the discharge in Holmes of his tightly held reserve.

The only falling out to have ever taken place between Holmes and Watson is documented in The Secret Adventure of the Piltdown Fossil; the ninth story in this series.

With the discovery of the Piltdown Man, in Sussex, in 1912, the scientific community is broadsided; while the mundane population is dumbfounded. A shift in the mind of the masses leads them to an epiphany on evolution.

When Dr. Arthur Conan Doyle is commissioned to investigate the Piltdown find, he enlists Dr. Watson as a collaborator. Watson travels to Sussex to meet with Dr. Doyle, and with Charles Dawson and Pierre Teilhard de Chardin; before all four visit the site. Holmes is left in the lurch until he is called in to analyze the Piltdown fossils; thanks to a clever intercession by Watson.

The final story, The Secret Adventure of the Irish Rising, is a tale which Holmes forbade the telling of, ever; not to be told for a millenium or two. I mean no dishonor to my lifelong friend, now deceased; but the pathos and sympathetic response engendered by the actual history involved, triggers a momentum whose time to surface is at hand.

The time is the spring season of 1916. Holmes receives an ambiguous telegram on Holy Thursday from his Irish cousin, inviting him to come over for an Easter visit. By the Saturday morning, Holmes is crossing the Irish Sea, from Holyhead in Wales to Dublin in Ireland; having departed as Sherlock Holmes and disembarked as Oscklehr Moshel, an itinerant gypsy.

Moshel/Holmes gets wind of the event hinted at in the telegram sent by his cousin Declan. Rumors are making the rounds of Dublin's pubs, divulged in lowly whispers and mumbles of patriotic inebriates.

There is a 'Rising' in the wind; the seminal event of each Irish generation. Torn asunder by his divided ancestry, Moshel/Holmes attempts to walk a line of demarcation between the forces of rebellion and the Sassenach.

The Secret Adventure of the Vanishing Marquis

Due to patriotic concerns, Mr. Sherlock Holmes forbade me to record in my journal certain of our shared adventures, especially several which had occured during the advent of the Great War.

"Some of our more sensitive escapades are best left for the time capsule of history, Watson. Not to be revealed for a century or more", said he on more than one occasion.

Yet, some mysterious, inner voice kept urging me to etch them in the pages of my mind. Although I was dubious in the beginning, I discovered that after I had composed the first adventure mentally, it remained in my memory. I was able to recall it at will. It was the same with subsequent stories in the confidential category mandated by Holmes. Some of which involved the highest levels of government; several involving the very survival of England!

I must apologize profusely to the reader for the deceptions in my previous writings, wherein I sent Sherlock Holmes under the Reichenbach Falls, in May 1891. Sending down the curtain on our association for three years. The exigencies of the times, along with Holmes' caveat, were paramount factors in my agreeing to relegate the final group of tales to clandestineness.

My disquietude increased as each secret adventure was composed in my immediate memory, however indelibly, lest these unseeable chronicles (except in my mind's eye) be lost with my eventual demise. But Holmes had other notions. For a remarkable bit of scientific information had come into his posession, by way of one of his intuitive flashes of perception.

Mrs. Hudson brought up a pot of tea shortly after admitting me to the premises. Holmes emerged to find me settled into the well-worn armchair by the fire. He curled into the chair opposite, tucking his blue dressing-gown about him.

"Watson, we have been ignoramuses!", he chided.

"Indeed!", I replied in a pique. "What, precisely have we been ignorant of?"

"Clairvoyance, Watson, clairvoyance: the ability to see beyond the senses. Have you heard of the clairvoyant in Poughkeepsie?"

I took a sip of tea while I composed myself.

"Come, come, Watson", he continued, bolting upright to fetch his black, clay pipe from the mantlepiece, "the makings of a new adventure is upon us." He sank back into the old armchair, puffing steadily, and retreated into meditation.

There was no way of telling how long Holmes would remain in the trance-like state that had become so familiar to me. A self-induced, meditative state that had proven instrumental in the inception of many of his deductions. I went to look out the bow window above Baker Street and found an obscure volume on the round table. Holmes had been reading about Andrew Jackson Davis, a clairvoyant in America, known as the Poughkeepsie Seer.

It had been a fortnight since our last adventure and Holmes was not immune to the vicissitudes of wishful thinking when eager to discover a new detection. In the pantheon of my understanding, I had assigned the concept of 'clairvoyance' to the cunning realm of fortune tellers, gipsy readers of crystal balls, and kindred aficionado of charlatanry.

Back by the fire I began to read on this extant sleuth in New York who had become a medical doctor in his sixties, after a life of altruistic clairvoyance. Fascinated, I read on in a timeless fashion, warming in the advancing sunlight. Holmes remained entranced until midday, when he sat upright and resumed drinking his cup of tea.

"What do you make of it?", he said, gesturing to the book in my hands.

"It's a convincing account", I replied.

"Your man, Davis, is indeed extraordinary", said Holmes, steepling his fingers and gazing upwards.

"So, you believe that he is truly clairvoyant?", I asked.

"It would ceratainly appear to be so", replied Holmes, pointing at the book; a remarkable narration of the ability to conduct the transfer of thought, while in an hypnotic trance."

"This is unlike you, Holmes, to readily accept the truth of a book, without any apprehension on your part."

"Let me say that I am more acquainted with mental telepathy than I have ever let on to you, Watson. But I'll say no more on this subject for now."

"I say, Holmes", I announced, "this chap, Davis, may still be living. He was born in 1826."

"He is eighty years of age and enjoying his retirement", said Holmes. The glint in his eyes signaled, as the lightning forespeaks the thunder, the mental elation he relished at the beginning of each new adventure.

Holmes arose and began pacing the room. He was at work again. The twin engines of deduction and logical synthesis were running in his analytical mind. After a while he stood before the fire, in a manner suggesting he had reached a conclusion of some kind, to lift a glowing turf with the tongs in order to relight his black pipe.

"You look like the cat that caught the canary", I quipped. After recording fifty-six of his adventures I knew when Holmes was amenable to a humorous remark.

"If you will permit me to respond to one maxim with another, I have come up with a plan to kill two birds with one stone", he retorted.

"What would the second stone entail?", I asked. "Assuming that the first involves the subject of clairvoyance, of course."

"For the time being, Watson, we shall relegate your question to the domain of rhetorical riddles."

I confess to a passing irritation in response to what I perceived to be the patronizing attitude Holmes sometimes exhibited toward me in these situations. My ultimate regard for my friend always trumped these untoward feelings before they could trigger any friction between us, however. Holmes always noticed, of course, usually choosing to let me dangle in the downdraft of my own disposition.

"Think, Watson!", he sang out. "Think back over the cases we have solved together. Now think back further, to those we have failed to resolve successfully. You know how it pains me to include the word 'failure' in my vernacular. In what type of case would a clairvoyant have been most helpful to us?"

By including me in his phrasing of case-solving, Holmes had intentionally assuaged my sensitive feelings; a first in our peerless partnership. I responded in my congenital, ingenuous manner.

Holmes had reclaimed his armchair in a cloud of contented pipe smoke.

"The cases involving missing persons never found", I said.

"Precisely, Watson. The Marquis of Marlbourough is still missing."

At that moment the front door bell rang downstairs. A few moments later, Mrs. Hudson entered after knocking.

"A telegram for you, sir", she said to Holmes.

"Mr. Andrew Jackson Davis has agreed to assist us, Watson", Holmes ejaculated. "The Poughkeepsie Seer may become the Rosetta Stone of detective work, with a not insignificant assist from Holmes and Watson."

The illumination in the eyes of my companion and friend glowed with a glistening never before observed from my perspective.

"Be a good fellow and retrieve the file on the Marlborough Marquis", proposed Holmes, as he left the sitting room, heading for the inner sanctum.

I selected the file in question from the row of filing cabinets in close proximity to the wall of bookcases opposite the fireplace; moved there by Holmes for the dual purpose of retaining the heat and of blocking the prevailing winds from the north; dampening both their sound and their fury.

There was no way of predicting the return of the great detective to my humble company, but on this singular occasion his sudden reappearance jolted me.

"Make haste, Watson, if you would accompany me", he cried, as he hurried to the coat rack to don his cloak.

"Where are we bound to?", I replied, hurrying after him.

"The London Library is our destination, Watson. *Tempus fugit.*"

We walked to the corner of Dorset where Holmes sounded his hansom whistle (two blasts) for a two-seater hansom cab, which promptly trotted us off; from Baker Street across Oxford, down to Bond, into St. James Square. The same route usually chosen by Holmes when he desired to contact the Baker Street Irregulars, many of whom's *locus standi* was among the costermongers on the east end of Oxford Street. Holmes had to remind the coachman to turn south on Bond Street, in order to reach our destination.

The conversation inside the cab departed from the desultory, spasmodic pattern of typical travellers, to focus on the detractious reputation often attributed to hypnotists and their craft.

"Your man in Poughkeepsie is hardly a mountebank," began Holmes. "Notwithstanding his cognizance of your *nulli secundis* hyperbole relating to my work, he has become expert in placing himself in a self-hypnotic trance. While in this sleep-like state, he becomes a channel for unprecedented excursions in clairvoyance."

I managed to surpress a smile into a simper concerning his facetious reference to my writing. Holmes continued.

"While self-hypnotized, Davis is questioned by a trusted assistant on one and sundry topics. No matter the theme, Davis answers all: from diagnosing medical conditions, to locating missing persons, to forecasting the future! His press clippings are astounding.

"His diagnoses of baffling medical conundrums, across untravelled distances and in unknown patients, strains the mental hold of even the most sane amongst us. Including myself!

"A third party to his readings is a trusted secretary, who makes a record of each session, in shorthand notation; from which she produces a transcript, using a typewriter."

"I shall most certainly have a keen interest in the medical diagnoses", I chimed in.

"As you have most likely surmised, we shall need a third party to assist with the experiment which I am devising. Preferably an intelligent woman who can record in shorthand. Perhaps Mrs. Watson would consider joining us, Watson?"

"I shall present the proposal to her, forthwith."

"Excellent, Watson!", replied Holmes.

We rode in silence the remaining distance to the library, whereupon Holmes dashed toward his favorite repository, before I re-routed the cab to my home on Queen Anne Street. During his hasty egress, he halloo'd that we meet back at Baker Street for afternoon tea. As I watched him disappear into his beloved library, fond memories of our past exploits arose to accompany me on the return trip. As Old Bond Street gave way to New Bond Street, the cab passed by the picture gallery involved in my recounting of the Hound of the Baskervilles case, before going by Madame Lesurier's milliner shop which played a role in my chronicle of the Silver Blaze adventure.

A realization came over me of the fraternal bonding that existed between Holmes and myself; a symbiosis impervious to absences or marriages. An indestructible partnership was one of the byproducts of our episodic work together. He as mentor; I as protege.

Crossing Oxford Street, the cab went by the building on Vere Street, where a falling brick nearly struck Holmes, in the tale I prematurely entitled the Final Problem. Rolling along, the cab entered Cavendish Square, the high rent district populated by many doctor residences, and a locale mentioned in several other of my narratives. Upon arrival at 323 Queen Anne Street, I paid the coachman and entered my wife's townhome; a stately residence which she so graciously shared with this penny-a-liner.

Truly my better half, consort, and goodwife, she replied in the affirmative straight away, eager to assist in any way the venerated Sherlock Holmes; for whom she held an incomparable esteem. She and I were of the proverbial one mind when it came to the inimitable Sherlock Holmes. So, she mizzled from my company, ostensibly to prepare for her new commission, whilst I took refuge behind the pocket doors of the residence study in order to fancy a nap.

At half-three, Mrs. Watson knocked me up to join her in a hansom cab waiting outside. We arrived at Baker Street in the West end some twenty minutes later. Mrs. Hudson greeted us effusively, kindly welcoming Mrs. Watson to the premises, before showing us upstairs.

Holmes was waiting at the doorway, having deaked our arrival from the window. He ushered us in and bade us welcome.

"I am jubilant to see you have decided to join us in the pursuit of the unknown, Mrs. Watson", Holmes beamed, as he gestured us to be seated. "I see that you can write in shorthand."

"Why, yes, I can, Mr. Holmes; but how would you know?"

"By the dimensions of your handbag, my dear. Too large to suit the dictates of Victorian fashion, but ample enough to conceal a stenographer's notebook."

"Well done, Holmes!", said I.

"Yes, bravo, Mr. Holmes. I have heard much on your talent for detection and have become an ardent admirer. To experience your ingenuity first-hand, however, causes a smile in my mind", gushed the goodwife.

"Harumph," was all I could say.

Holmes looked resplendent in his finest robe and slippers as he posed at the fireplace, one hand on the mantlepiece, one in his righthand pocket. He was slyly warming himself, an indication (using his very own powers of observation and deduction) that he had been in the unheated alcove for some time, just prior to our arrival. He was smiling like the Cheshire cat.

At four o'clock, Mrs. Hudson came in carrying a great tray brimming with the components of a formal high tea, including: sandwiches, scones, Devon Cream, jams, fruit, and assorted cakes, along with a teapot brought back from the Crimea by her great-uncle, who served with the Cameron Highlanders.

Holmes used the occasion to inform us of his plan at hand. He proceeded to speak in a low-keyed tone of voice, an uncharacteristic style which was undoubtedly due to the presence of a lady. For all his powers of reason, he could be overawed in the presence of a woman. Despite his assertion to 'have never loved', he was not immune to female pulchritude. At several junctures (involving scintillating women) his esteem for a beautiful female resembled a case of Platonic love. I refer, for instance, to his regard for Irene Adler (recorded in the Adventure in Bohemia story), notwithstanding his defeat at her hand.

We had consumed the sandwiches and were enjoying the cakes. The point in time of a High Tea when a fellow feeling of chummyness often enters the company.

Holmes began to speak after a period of silence.

"Precisely at five o'clock London time I will enter an hypnotic trance. Mr. Andrew Jackson Davis has agreed to do likewise at the corresponding time in Poughkeepsie, New York.

"I have here a list of questions for you to ask of me, Watson, once I have put myself into a deep sleep. You will record all said, Mrs. Watson, both questions and answers. Mr. Davis and his team will perform a similar experiment.

"In the meantime, while you two muzz the procedure, I shall prepare myself."

Then he absconded to his bedroom, after handing me two lists written in his own hand.

The one list, headed 'Poughkeepsie', had the following questions:

1. Have you any knowledge of Sherlock Holmes?
2. Can you locate him, presently?
3. Are you able to discern his current mental state, including his most pressing problem?
4. Is there a denouement in the offing?

The second list was headed 'London', and had these questions:

A. Have you any knowledge of the Poughkeepsie Seer?
B. Can you recall the case of the Marquis of Marlborough?
C. Has Scotland Yard made any progress in an effort solve the disappearance of the Marquis?
D. Can you locate the missing Marquis?

Holmes reappeared at four fifty-five. His final remark dealt with the timing of the four questions; which were to begin at five fifteen, continue in five minute intervals, and complete at half-five.

At five o'clock, half-reclining on the fainting chair, he closed his eyes and remained motionless, as if fast asleep. Mrs. Watson and I sat in the armchairs that had been pre-positioned: mine at the head of Holmes' lounge; her's at the foot.

I had some time to peruse the two lists during which an inkling of a congruence arose in my consciousness. Then the clock on the mantle chimed the quarter-hour, whereupon I read the first question aloud.

"The exploits in question are well-known to the entity," came an answer from Holmes.

I looked at Mrs. Watson while she was writing in her notebook. Done, she nodded to me. We remained in silence.

I read aloud the second question at five-twenty.

Came a response in the same monotone: "The entity present attempted to solve the mystery involved with the disappearance, but failed."

We had been admonished by Holmes to remain silent during the five-minute intervals between questions. We complied, of course. At five twenty-five I read aloud the third.

"Scotland Yard, always reticent, has a clandestine category for cases that meet particular criteria. Secrecy is never more critical to the Yard than when their own reputation is involved." Once again, an answer spoken in an unreasoning monotone by Holmes.

We both sat in silence after hearing this curious response. It took a pointing gesture by me to remind my wife to record the answer. Soon the half-hour chimed. I read aloud the fourth question.

"'Missing' is a matter of conjecture. One man's found is another man's lost. The whereabouts of your man, the royal in abscondence, can be determined by another."

After another interval, I woke Holmes via a pre-arranged signal. He sprang to his feet.

"May I see the transcript, Mrs. Watson?"

"Certainly, Mr. Holmes," she replied.

As Holmes contemplated the responses to the questions, with furrowed brow and steady gaze, I found myself also pondering the happenings of the past half-hour.

Was a telepathic connection established between Holmes and the clairvoyant? Did Holmes have an innate psychic nature, or sixth sense, that manifested itself in his remarkable ability to logicize? Was this the source of his genius?

These, along with other questions, lead me to a conclusion. Namely, that there was more to this seance than meets the eye.

"There has been some telepathy here!", said Holmes suddenly. "These answers of mine, of which I have no conscious recall of reciting, indicate an extrasensory perception has supervened." That said, he walked over to the fireplace to fetch a pipe.

"My God!", I ejaculated, "What have we done?"

"Calm yourself, Watson," he replied, "for these are very deep waters we are wading into."

Seemingly unperturbed, my goodwife addressed us baith.

"Shall I assume that my services are no longer required this evening?", she inquired.

"By all means, my dear", said Holmes. "Thank you; you have been of material assistance to me."

Turning to me he directed that I summon a cab for Mrs. Watson, down in front. Upon her departure I was to return upstairs at once; which I did.

I returned the hansom cab whistle to the shelf over the hat rack, behind the entrance door. Holmes was pacing the floor.

"Any views, Watson?", he asked.

"Well, Holmes, I must confess that I am taken aback by what seems to have taken place. Were you being perfectly candid when you professed unconsciousness, or were you play acting for some scheme or experiment of your own?"

"The trace of paranoia in your question is to be expected, I suppose", Holmes answered, "considering the subjects at hand. Clairvoyance, telepathy, and hypnosis are not disciplines for the faint of heart."

"Were you truly in an hypnotic trance?", I implored.

"I was, Watson," he asserted, "I truly was."

"Very well, Holmes. I trust you understand my incredulity."

"Indeed," he replied.

"As for my views, if any; my thoughts are running a gauntlet between rational observation and novel nuance. Yet the phrase 'royal in abscondence' bespoke a new, or re-opened case for Sherlock Holmes; in my opinion."

"Excellent, Watson! Your intuition also bespeaks. It tells of your innate intelligence. Next we must meet with Inspector LeStrade tomorrow morning in Scotland Yard. I will depend on you to meet me here in the morning."

By nine o'clock the next morning we were riding to the Yard in a hansom cab in a mist of rain. I decided to draw Holmes out by a continuation of the conversation of the previous evening, which had been abbreviated.

"Why did you have me pull the file on the Marquis of Marlborough yesterday? Why not one of the other missing persons on file?"

"An astute question, my friend. A clear indication that you recognized the genre of wrongdoing which could most benefit from the forte of a clairvoyant.

"Of the score of missing person incidents remaining to be solved by Scotland Yard, the case of the Marquis is the *terra incognita*. What better subject quarry for the *sui generis* mysticism we have been involved with since yesterday?

"At the time of the alleged disappearance - presumeably down a bog hole while hunting - two items of fact insinuated themselves in the repository of my suspicion. Firstly, the Marquis had never before hunted with his companion on the hunt; secondly, he had never before hunted in that locale."

"And what were you able to deduce from such meager details?", I asked sceptically.

"Enough to suspect foulplay of some sort. The Marquis had fought the Boers in South Africa. He was proficient in hunting and fishing. He had ridden with the hounds on many a fox hunt; too many to vanish on a bogland moor. He was a cousin to Sir Winston Churchill. Men of his character and achievment seldom, if ever, meet their demise due to an egregious incompetency on their part. Yes, I know it remains a possibility, but the odds against it are mind-boggling. Which leaves me with the penultimate unbelief in his apparent accidental death."

"What do you expect to learn from Inspector LeStrade this

morning?", I asked, with rising interest.

"Something, anyway, Watson," he replied, and then paused in mid-thought, before continuing.

"My third answer while under hypnosis referred to a clandestine category of cases at Scotland Yard. I have long surmised this to be so, but have never spoken of it with you. Yet, I have discussed it with my brother, Mycroft, who is convinced of the Yard's passion for concealment whenever it suits their purposes."

"This would account for your inclusion of a question about Scotland Yard on your list of questions, I suppose."

"Precisely, Watson. Let us pray that LeStrade will provide the key to this secret arcanum."

The cab pulled into the Yard after travelling through Trafalgar Square and south on Whitehall.

Upstairs, on the second floor, LeStrade had received a note from Holmes, and was expecting us. LeStrade met us with a smug grin. The great Sherlock Holmes was coming to call, hat in hand, he hoped.

"Come in, Holmes! Good morning, Dr. Watson."

"Likewise, Inspector," said Holmes.

"Good morning to you, Inspector," said I.

"How may I help you?" said LeStrade, pompously.

"Kindly close the door," said Holmes to me.

Then he spoke to LeStrade.

"We have come on a matter of the utmost importance. A life or death situation involving a member of the aristocracy. You, LeStrade, are the only man in England who can help me solve this remarkable case."

"Certainly, Holmes, please sit down. How can I be of assistance?" replied LeStrade, now smiling broadly.

"It is imperative that the Yard re-open the Marlborough investigation. New evidence has surfaced which has the potential to bring this case back-to-life, so to speak."

The Inspector's facial expression began to metamorphize; from a broad smile to an inquisitive smirk.

"The Marquis is dead, Holmes! He perished in the bog.

What more is there to say?"

The Inspector was being setup for a knockout blow.

"Disappearance cases are most extraordinary," said Holmes. "They present an unprecedented array of possibilities, my dear fellow. Minus *habeus corpus*, for example, it is conceivable that the man lives, is it not?"

The trap was sprung. Could LeStrade resist the chance to prove the great Sherlock Holmes wrong?

"'Conceivable' does not feed the bulldog, Holmes. There is some indication that the Marquis' departure may have been a suicide," said LeStrade, pouncing on his chance to outwit Sherlock Holmes.

"Aha!" exclaimed Holmes, "I have taken the precaution to bring my file on the case, containing every clipping from the Telegraph and from the Chronicle, pertaining to the alleged disappearance in question. There was never any hint or suggestion of felo-dese in these newspaper columns.

"However, the precepts of logic state there is some piece of evidence in your file on the case, which would prompt you to express your mention of 'some indication' of self-destruction. You would never have volunteered such a ground-breaking opinion without some hard evidence to buttress your claim. You are too good a detective to have done less, Lestrade."

LeStrade's expression descended into glumness. He looked like a schoolboy brought before the headmaster.

"I am a good detective. The best in Scotland Yard. Why, you said so yourself, Holmes, on several occasions. But you misled me by coming in here claiming 'a life or death' situation concerning someone I know to be dead."

"Holmes did say 'life OR death'," I interjected.

"Exactly!" said Holmes. "Perhaps, LeStrade, you will now reveal the evidence by which you believe the Marquis to be deceased."

The Inspector rose from his chair behind the desk and walked over to the window overlooking Victoria Embankment. He spoke while gazing outwards.

"We three go aways back, we do. Did you know what my colleagues here at the Yard call us? They refer to us as the 'Three Musketeers of Scotland Yard'. You two have become trusted companions, my closest comrades in crime-solving."

At this point he turned to face us and then continued his colloquy.

"The Marquis of Marlborough left a suicide note. The King, himself, asked the Yard to hugger-mugger it. It wouldn't do for a royal, cousin to the King, to have done away with himself. So, we obliged the Royal Family and concealed the suicide note from the public domain. If somehow this evasion were to become public knowledge, Scotland Yard would disavow the existence of any such letter."

"I must see the note!" shouted Holmes, leaping to his feet.

"Very well, Holmes," replied LeStrade, in a muted voice, as he retired to an inner office.

When he returned, he handed a letter to Holmes, which read as follows.

To My Family:

I am wearing my Norfolk jacket for the last time. For, I am off to join our renowned ancestors in oblivion.

"Let not the wails becoming to accompany my soul as it retreats one last time to a self-imposed extinction."

The Marquis of Marlborough

Holmes had me copy it before returning the letter to the Inspector. We left without further ado.

Once outside Scotland Yard, we hailed another hansom cab and directed it to 221 Baker Street. Holmes began to scrutinize the letter. After passing through Oxford Circus we were proceeding along Oxford Street, when he looked up at me suddenly.

"Any final views, Watson?"

"The poetic suicide note generates a pathos in me for everyone whose lives have been impacted by this tragedy," I began, somewhat pompously, I'm afraid. "The one illuminating aspect of this case, a case that can now be moved to your closed file, has been your palaver with hypnosis. Some measure of telepathy was apparently experienced which may be instrumental in resurrecting other unsolved cases being held in abeyance," I pontificated.

Holmes held his tongue for the rest of the trip.

When we arrived at 221 Baker Street, he leaped from the cab, calling back to me as he reached the front steps. "The Marquis of Marlborough is alive and well, living in a monastery in Wales!" Then he disappeared into the premises.

Flabbergsted, I directed the coachman to Queen Anne Street, where a brandy was waiting to comfort me.

When next we met, my chagrin was the catalyst that prompted Holmes to assuage my incomprehension. It was my silence at breakfast that gave me away.

"You're as quiet as a church mouse, Watson. Why haven't you pelted me with questions about the Marquis?"

As usual, his question went to the crux of the matter.

"For the love of me, Holmes," I began, already feeling better, "how can you say that the Marquis is still alive?"

Holmes stood and went for a pipe on the mantle. He lit up the black briar and came back to his armchair.

"Do you have your notebook?" he asked.

"I do," I said, opening to the Marquis' suicide note.

"Consider the very first sentence, Watson," Holmes began, "why bother to mention that one is giving up 'hunting', if one is planning to commit suicide?

"Now look at the second sentence. He is going to 'oblivion', which my dictionary defines as 'the condition or fact of being forgotten'. One's demise is not a prerequisite in order to be forgotten.

"Next is the four-line verse, which is imperspicuous, and redolant of a cryptograph. The gist of this poem comes across to the casual reader as a gestalt for suicide. On the other hand, a discriminative analysis suggests otherwise.

"Namely, I became certain that the Marquis had encoded a message, within the verse, for his loved ones. The first word in the second sentence was incongruous to the sentence; thus becoming suspect. The word 'For' being homonymous with the 'four' in four-line verse.

"One of the simpler coding techniques consists of word positioning within the envelope message. If we read only every fourth word in verse, we have:

'Wails my retreats to extinction.'

"Once one assumes a message within, 'wails' easily becomes 'Wales', or 'Wales is'. The term 'retreats' can be read 'retreat', or 'retreat is'. My preferred meaning is:

Wales is my retreat to extinction.

"The next target of my scrutiny was the term 'extinction'. Does not this usage translate into a long, slow process, when examined by an average reader? As opposed to the terms 'demise', or 'expiration', which would signify death. Lastly, we have 'retreat' which can mean 'to go into a retirement for religious devotion'.

"My final conclusion could only be that which I so cavalierly called out as I ran from the hansom last evening: The Marquis of Marlborough is alive and living in a monastery in Wales!"

The Secret Adventure of the Psychic Connection

It was during the early part of September in 1911 that an episode occurred which involved the highest levels of government, the first in a series of adventures designated top secret by both parties; 10 Downing Street and Sherlock Holmes.

Responding to a note from Holmes which had been delivered to my town home the previous evening by one of the Baker Street Irregulars, I arrived at 221 Baker Street by 10 o'clock the next morning.

Holmes was just returning from his morning ramble through the West End and saluted my hansom cab with a wave of his alpenstock, the walking stick presented to him in gratitude by a minor noble in Transylvania. His demeanor was clear and brisk, a match for the autumnal morning.

Mrs. Hudson had the tea waiting. Once upstairs, we took our respective armchairs at the fireside. The banked turf fire kept the damp chill from intruding. We began reading our preferred evening newspapers, Holmes the Times, me the Telegraph, while sipping our tea.

"I say, Watson," said Holmes from behind his paper, "the gods of war are rising from their slumber, I'm afraid!"

I gave a start of surprise.

"Why on earth would you say that?" I asked.

"Do you recall the Agadir Incident in July?" he asked.

"I do, of course. The German gunboat taking position in the Mediterranean, off North Africa."

"The War Minister, Lord Haldane, has built up an Expeditionary Force," Holmes expounded. "The First Lord of the Admiralty has proposed the Force be abandoned. This battle-of-titans looming can only be resolved by the Prime Minister."

"What do you expect will happen?" I asked, noticing the gleam in my friend's steel, grey eyes.

"One of the Lords will get the sack. Like as not McKenna at the Admiralty. If this should come to pass, Asquith will be wise and select Churchill to head the Admiralty."

"Sir Winston Spenser Churchill would hardly be my choice, Holmes. Back in '06, he and Lloyd George led the attack on a naval armament bill in Parliament. He has since opposed a strong Army and Navy and has recently acquired the sobriquet, 'The Little Englander'."

"Precisely why we shall have our work cut out for us, Watson, if we are to steer the ship of England in perilous times!"

"Holmes, you astound me!" I ejaculated. "What on earth can you be speaking of?"

"Have you forgotten our secret weapon, Watson? Remember our sojourn to Poughkeepsie?"

"Once does not forget a once in a lifetime experience," I replied, a little put out by the implication.

Just then, Mrs. Hudson brought up the morning Telegraph. The front page confirmed Holmes' presumption: Sir Winston Spenser Churchill had been appointed First Lord of the Admiralty, replacing Reginald McKenna. I handed the newspaper to Holmes.

"Once again my sources have been prescient. These unnamed and unsung loyalists have been essential to our pursuits, Watson. One day you must make mention of them, kindly, in your memoirs."

"Pray, when shall I be free to mention your unnamed sources, of which I have a profound ignorance?" I asked, tongue-in-cheekily.

"All in good time, my friend," he responded, with smiling eyes bedeviling his attempt to dismiss my moxie. "Meanwhile, we have the safety of the British Navy in our sights. Are you *animis opibusque parati* to come on board?"

"*Semper paratus*!" said I.

"Excellent reply. Sometimes a rhetorical question deserves an answer, signally in the Latin.

"We have before us what may readily be considered a turning point in British history. We have recently turned the page on a century of British dominion on the high seas; an age when the sun never set on the British Empire! In the first decade of the new century, we the English have been dismantling our sea power; while, they the Germans have been generating a navy that may have reached a parity with our own.

"One of the leading proponents of the build-down of our military is now in charge of our navy. He is a good man of high character and sound intellect, but he is the son of one of the leading Liberal politicians in recent history. Although, his faithful adherence to his father's views has been slowing eroding since Sir Winston's appointment as Home Secretary in 1910. He has shown himself to be a man of ideas, who also is comfortable with command."

"He led a cavalry charge against the Dervishes in Egypt, as a young lieutenant, in the Sudan, under Kitchner," I interjected.

"Ripping recollection,Watson. Yes, and as a young reporter in South Africa he managed to escape from the Boers after being taken prisoner. His is the personification of the English character."

"Bravo, Holmes. Brilliant accolade."

Holmes went to look out the window before continuing. "I am expecting a reply to my message to the First Lord of the

Admiralty, which was delivered early this morning. Sir Winston is on intimate political terms with my brother, Mycroft. I am confidant that my request for an audience will be honored."

"Will I be included?" I asked.

"Categorically, Watson. Can you drop everything and come a running? (As they say in the American West.) When we learn of our being granted a meeting?"

"When duty calls I shall be ready," I asserted.

While Holmes read the newspaper, I had a nap. One of the street Arabs arrived, with a reply from the Admiralty Building in Whitehall, within the hour.

The note read as follows:

Mr. Sherlock Holmes:

The timing of your congratulatory message exceptional in that it preceded the announcement of my new appointment. I suppose one should expect no less from the world's greatest detective.

As for the matter at hand, one of the utmost secrecy, kindly be at my offices at 10 A.M. tomorrow morning. You shall have my undivided attention for the hour.

Very Sincerely Yours,
Winston Churchill
First Sea Lord

I must admit to an inner excitement at the prospect of a private meeting with Mr. Churchill; yet outwardly I was unable to react sanguinely. Holmes quite naturally detected my loss of homeostasis. Once again he left it for me to be hoisted on my own petard.

"If I assume that we shall be conducting an experiment in clairvoyance, for the benefit of the First Sea Lord, will I ask Mrs. Watson to be available?" I asked.

"No need, Watson. Yes, we will be demonstrating what is possible under hypnosis, but any recording of the confidential event is best left to the private secretary of Lord Churchill."

"Forgive my skepticism, Holmes, but why do I receive the significant impression that there is more to this pending situation than you have conveyed to me?"

"Be patient, my good friend. The very survival of English freedom...," Holmes hesitated mid-sentence to permit the rising patriotic feeling to pass, "...may rest in our hands."

I directed the hansom cab to stop by 221 Baker Street the next morning in order to pick up a Mr. Sherlock Holmes, before continuing on to Whitehall. The coachman, one Fergus O' Finnegan of the County Fermaugh, introduced himself. Fergus confided to me that he was one of Mr. Holmes' regular drivers.

The doorman at the Admiralty escorted us to the offices of the First Sea Lord. Sir Winston was waiting in his inner office, seated behind a great mahogany desk in a warmly paneled room overlooking St. James Park. He welcomed us graciously.

"The renowned brother of Mycroft Holmes; I am most pleased to welcome you and your learned friend, Dr. John Watson."

"Likewise, Sir Winston," replied Holmes. "We are most thankful for this audience. We come in urgency!"

"I have read the material which you sent to me, as per your request, in order to be prepared for today's experiment. The notion of clairvoyance has the burden of proof in this theater, however. I disclose this bias to you before we begin," responded Sir Winston.

"One would expect nothing less from a man in your exalted position, and in such ominous times," said Holmes.

Only then, when they both paused to look toward me did I mutter some inconsequential remark, which went unanswered by the two titans.

Each of us present had a hidden agenda. Mine was the simplest and least devious. I had a list of questions, composed by

Holmes, to be asked of him while he was in the trance of self-hypnosis.

Holmes and I expected Sir Winston to ignore the session protocol, which dictated only one questioner, by injecting himself into the demonstration as a second interrogator.

Holmes entertained levels of thought and intuition that were known only to him and his brother and several others in England. One could never be sure of the plans and schemes of Sherlock Holmes.

Holmes put himself into a self-hypnotic trance at 10:15 A.M. The First Sea Lord followed the protocol and joined me in silence. At 10:30 A.M., I prepared to read the first question on my list aloud to a dormant, deep-breathing Holmes.

Meanwhile, at an undisclosed location in New York, Andrew Jackson Davis, the Poughkeepsie Seer, had hypnotized himself at the corresponding time in America. The pair of synchronous somnambulants were departing for some far away shore, sailors on an unknown sea, in the service of Christendom and Western Civilization.

There was to be a one minute interval between the paired questioning in London and New York. So, at 10:30 A.M. London time, the first question was asked of the Poughkeepsie Seer in New York.

"Have you any knowledge of Sir Winston Churchill?"

"The entity is the son of Lord Randolph Churchill," came an answer from the sleeping Davis.

At precisely 10:31 A.M. London time, the first question was put to the sleeping Sherlock Holmes in London, by myself.

"Are you able to contact the Poughkeepsie Seer?"

Holmes answered in a low monotone voice.

"The mystic is currently observing those of us present."

The second pair of questions was to begin at 10:40 A.M. The original fifteen minute interval between each question, to each hypnotic, had been reduced to a ten minute interval for this seance, in deference to Churchill's legendary impatience. But once again, the new First Sea Lord remained silent, as I did.

At 10:40 A. M. the second question on the New York list was read aloud to the Poughkeepsie Seer in New York.

"Are you able to locate Sir Winston Churchill?"

"The entity is at his office in the Admiralty, in London," came an answer from Davis.

The New York session was being recorded by a trusted stenographer and being conducted by a trusted assistant.

So as not to miss a murmur, a mutter, or a mumble, Sir Winston sat forward and leaned into the circle around Holmes. At 10:41 A.M. I read the second question aloud.

"Are you able to discern a future event, like an impending war in Europe?"

Again, a low monotone voice emitted from Holmes.

"Yes, a war in Europe is inevitable; the storm clouds are gathering on the horizon."

The First Sea Lord was knocked back upright in his chair by this answer. For the next nine minutes he paced around the room. In New York, the third question was read at 10:50 A.M. sharp.

"Are you able to discern his current mental state, including his most pressing problem?"

"Although the new head of the Admiralty is singularly clear-headed, he is now preoccupied with the safety of the British Navy," came the answer.

In London, the third question came at exactly 10:51 A.M.

"Will the impending war in Europe involve the British Empire?"

"By sea, land, and air. The subject people will be drawn in to a colossal struggle on the continent," came the answer in drone.

The final question in New York was put to the Poughkeepsie Seer at precisely 11:00 A.M. (London time).

"What will be the fate of the British Navy with Churchill at the helm?"

"The entity would do well to monitor the Teuton," was the cryptic answer from Davis.

The fourth question in London came at 11:01 A.M.

"Will England and its Navy prevail?"

"The new First Sea Lord must look to a predecessor whereby the Navy can be recast for a superior performance," came the answer in drone.

This last answer set Churchill in motion. He stepped between myself seated and the reclining Holmes and spoke out his own question.

"What is the capacity of, and location of the German fleet?"

"The foreign fleet has the means and intention to blockade their greatest naval rival," was the answer.

Mrs. Hudson admitted me at mid-morning the following day. Proceeding upstairs, the sounds of violin playing greeted me. I entered his rooms and took my seat at the concert. He was playing Beethoven's *Ode To Joy,* with a virtuosity previously unknown to me. My companion's facial expressions indicated emotional levels of bliss, joy, and contentment hitherto concealed within his enigmatic personalty.

The morning newspaper was lying partly opened on the round table. The headline blared out, FLEET ALERTED. The new First Sea Lord, on his first morning in office, had ordered the entire British Navy to alert status. Battle squadrons were steaming eastward across the North Sea to blockade by patrol, Germany's outlets to deep water. A cordon was being set in place around the British Isles. All our submarines were out to sea.

As Holmes continued to play, I observed a solitary tear slowly descending his cheek. The lump in my throat prevented me from commenting.

Editor's Note:

When war broke out in August of 1914, the British Navy was ready to do battle. Under Churchill's leadership the entire

Navy had been changed over to oil, from coal. Her big guns had been increased to fifteen inch diameters from thirteen-point-five inches. A naval War Staff had been formed. In a new war room in the Admiralty, hung a chart of the North Sea showing the up to date positions of the German Navy. Britannia ruled the seas!
End Note.

The Secret Adventure of Irish Gunrunning

"Tell me, Watson," said Holmes, pausing from a morning reverie involving his chemical apparatus and the search for a non-addictive palliative, "will the winds of March diminish by St. Patrick's Day?"

Holmes had spent the past week indoors at 221 Baker Street, inside his flat, with only occasional jaunts down to Mrs. Hudson's for an evening meal. He abhorred the strong winds of the month of March, preferring instead the comfort of a warm fire.

I was absorbed in the morning newspaper, but I managed to mutter, "I imagine so." Then we resumed our respective pursuits, in silence.

At 10 A. M., Mrs. Hudson came up with a tray and announced the arrival of the letter alongside the pot of tea. As Holmes opened the letter, I cut open a blueberry scone and began to butter it. Holmes added some milk to his tea with one hand, while he read with the other. His eyes began to brighten with the luster that was usually the harbinger of the beginning of a new adventure. For despite my friend's disdain for my show of emotion, this was one physiological response outside the control of his intellect.

"It's from the Prime Minister, himself!" said Holmes, passing the letter to me.

The letter read as follows.

Thursday
July 16, 1914

Mr. Sherlock Holmes:

I trust this letter finds you and your associate, Dr. John Watson, hale and hearty. A matter is at hand of pivotal importance, involving the security of these British Isles. Imperative you Come to Downing Street as soon as possible.

Prime Minister Asquith
10 Downing Street

"Come Watson," called Holmes as he flew to the entrance door. *"Tempus fugit!"*

I quickly followed his run down the stairs and into the street. Two shrill blasts from his cab whistle brought a hansom at the brisk trot. We arrived at 10 Downing Street (forthwith) by 11 A. M.

The Prime Minister received us in his private anteroom off the large sitting room on the first floor. The acoustics of the small room were impeccably muffled by heavy drapery, hanging tapestries and deep carpeting.

"I have summoned you here to recognize your love of country," began Asquith, "as evidenced by your past services to our nation. Now that we, the British people, are being buffeted by winds of war emanating from the land of our Teutonic cousins; I must once again turn to you and call upon you in the name of his Majesty, the King.

"As you know, for the past three years my government has supported Home Rule for the whole of Ireland. The stumbling block in the situation has been the Province of Ulster. The Protestant Unionists are clamoring for civil war if Ulster should be given over to the control of a Catholic-dominated, one Ireland."

Holmes added, "'Home rule is Rome rule!" has become the battle cry in Ulster.

The Prime Minister continued. "Sunday last, 12 July, was the anniversary of the Battle of the Boyne. The annual victory parade was augmented by contraband rifles being shouldered by thousands of marchers for the Orange. These rifles had been recently smuggled into the country by ship.

"The north of Ireland has become a powder keg, threatening England's rear in any upcoming hostilities in Europe. The south of Ireland is becoming unnerved by the sabre-rattling in Ulster. Dublin has been petrified by the thousand rifles marching in Londonderry last Sunday.

"Meanwhile, one of our intelligence agents in Dublin has descried a plot to bring a shipment of rifles to arm the Irish Volunteers. Rumor has it a German ship will deliver the contraband cargo to the west coast of Ireland.

"The extreme urgency of this impending crisis dictates the calling in of our best. Thus, the incomparable sleuth and his right-hand man have been summoned to serve King and country.

"His Majesty and I personally entreat you to do all in your power to deflate, defuse, or diminish this time-bomb in Ireland."

Holmes responded immediately. "By all means, Prime Minister! The king wills it!"

By mid-afternoon we were on a train crossing the English Midlands, bound for the ferry to Dublin at Holyhead in Wales. The refreshment cart was a welcome sight rolling up the aisle. We enjoyed a semi-high tea of small sandwiches, jams, cakes, and fruit, along with the requisite pot of hot tea.

Before leaving from Euston Station in London, we had each managed to send off a telegram; Holmes to Dublin, Watson to his goodwife.

The sandwich cart colporteur, formerly a pushcart entrepreneur in St. James Park and one of the legion of Holmes' contacts in and about London, was delighted to be in the presence of his distinguished preceptor and recited for us the timetable regarding the ferry service between Holyhead and Dublin.

We settled back in our seats, Holmes by the window and myself on the aisle. The window seat opposite my friend was unoccupied, but riding backwards always made me vertiginous.

The midlands were in the full bloom of summer, with purple heather everywhere. Holmes was making entries in his pocket notebook, recording species of passing flowers and plants. As we proceeded west by northwest, the village life of England, a millennium in becoming, rolled by, neatly.

Entering Wales, one cannot fail to notice; due mainly to the many pastel colored designs and motifs hand-painted on the homes. The train makes about a sixty degree right turn to run due north to Holyhead along a track bed, lying between the Irish Sea coast and a spiny mountain ridge.

The ferry terminal at Holyhead encompasses a theater-sized hall that is the waiting room; a massive echo chamber wherein each footstep resounds inside the domed roof. The main portal into England for all too many Irish coming over to find work. My ancestry is Scottish and there are many Watsons in Ulster. I wondered to myself whether the trail we were seeking would lead us to Belfast in the north of Ireland.

We made a windy crossing over the Irish Sea on the evening ferry. At one point I observed Holmes passing a note to the vendor behind the fish and chips counter, whereby they engaged in an exchange of whispers. Holmes had enlisted another recruit in the war against crime, with the assistance of the note from the sandwich seller on the train.

Landing at 11 P.M., we walked to a nearby hostel, where once again, Holmes passed a note, this time to the hosteler. After spending a restful night, in the morning we enjoyed a private breakfast with the proprietor before setting out for the center of Dublin in a brisk breeze.

I had been enjoying the journey so completely as to have put aside my usual probing of the mental machinations of Sherlock Holmes. Choosing instead to engage my erudite friend in subjects of conversation which focused upon the vicissitudes of the trip.

"Holmes," I said, "here we are walking into Dublin, no less, and I have hardly a notion of what we are up to."

"Forgive me, Watson," he replied. "I thought you would realize I would begin our quest in Ireland with a call on my distant cousin, Declan O'Dempsey."

I stopped walking, causing Holmes to stop and turn to face me.

"For the love of God, Holmes, are you telling me you're Irish?"

"Only a wee bit, on me mother's side," he replied with smiling eyes, a roguish grin and an 'Oirish' brogue."

After pausing for my laugh, he continued.

"One of only a few Irish clan chiefs to defeat the English champion, Strongbow, in battle was The O'Dempsey."

"Your skills in pugilism will no longer amaze me," I replied as we resumed walking.

Declan O'Dempsey met us at the HalfPenny Bridge in the heart of downtown Dublin. He was all fire and brimstone; with sky blue eyes, narrow face and (carrot) red hair; angular limbs; in his mid-thirties.

"*Dia dhuit*, cousin Sherlock," said Declan.

"*Dia dhuit*, cousin Declan," replied Holmes.

"I got yer message, to meet you here, and I am here now on time, ammint I?"

"Your promptness is noteworthy. The more so due to the urgency of our mission. This is my associate, Dr. John Watson. We are traveling under the imprimatur of the King Of England. Your advocacy for Home rule has long been known to me. Your propinquity to those whose only passion is to see freedom rising in Ireland is the catalyst for my come around."

"Cousin Sherlock, my 'pink witty' is at your disposal."

"Your 'wit' has many colors, dear cousin. It can also serve as a camouflage in a difficult situation, such as the one we find before us. I speak, as you may have surmised, of the recent gunrunning into Ulster. A British intelligence agent here in Dublin has heard rumors of a planned counterstroke shipment of arms into the south of Ireland; a tit for tat gunrunning. I must know what you know of this, dear cousin Declan."

"Ever since those thousand rifles were landed in the north, all the chat has been of the lack of arms here in the south. I know of no specifics, but I do know a name that will surely be involved in any scheming to arm the Dublin brigade - who have been drilling with wooden guns."

"Pray tell," I blurted out, "for King and Country, give us the name."

"His name is Roger Casement," said Declan.

Declan O'Dempsey melded back into the tenement class of the city. We crossed over the river Liffey, turned left to walk alongside the river until O'Connell Bridge, where we turned right and strolled to Trinity College.

We walked onto Trinity ground through the main entrance, past the posting notices display cases on the left, and crossing the great, open quadrangle before locating the student and faculty commons. While I enjoyed the collegial ambiance and a pot of tea, Holmes went off to explore the premises, ostensibly. I found him afterwards in the university library, where I knew, of course, his peregrination of the grounds would deliver him.

"Well, Watson," said Holmes, from a chair at a reading table, "it appears that your man, Roger Casement, is a main figure in the acquisition of guns for the Dublin Volunteers."

"How on earth did you arrive at such a conclusion, and in so short a period of time?" I asked.

"Casement is someone to be reckoned with, a man of class and distinction. As we speak, he is on a passenger liner steaming toward New York. His final destination involves raising funds from an Irish-American organization, most probably in either Boston, New York, or Philadelphia. He has made previous sailings. I have just examined the passenger lists in the Ship's Registry."

"Very clever, indeed," I responded, "but what leads you to the conclusion that he is raising funds?"

"Simply the law of probability, Watson. For what other good reason would a man involved in gunrunning, leave the country during a time when Ulster is spoiling for a civil war? He is seeking money for guns; guns which can be shipped from a country much nearer to Ireland than America is. Money which is all too available from the legions of Irish in America."

"Your deductions and inductions never fail to amaze me, Holmes. However, are we now at an impasse until Mr. Casement returns?"

"Hardly a word I would choose in this instance. Not after my near demise at Reichenback Falls; that was an impasse. While we await his return we are free to seek him out in his domain."

"What is it you have in mind?" I asked.

"This island of Ireland has been dominated by England for over seven hundred years. The Irish have developed 'rising up against the oppressor' into an art form. They have traditionally been led and instigated by the intellectuals among them.

"Now that England is facing a probable coming war in Europe, the chances of the Irish planning another 'rising' approach certainty. We may further deduce that the coming rising has some of its roots planted on university grounds. Therefore we may conclude that your man, Roger Casement, has connections on this campus. It would not surprise me if the next rising is led by a professor."

"Your logic is impeccable, Holmes," I said. "Yet we are in the enemy camp, so to speak; who here will volunteer any information to a couple of Englishman?"

"Come along, my friend," said Holmes, as he rose from the chair. "We passed a bulletin board when we walked under the entrance archway leading into Trinity."

We re-crossed the quadrangle and stopped before the glass-enclosed posting boards in the entrance way. Messages and notes were posted in abundance inside the glass covered display enclosures.

"Let us learn what we can from this cornucopia of miscellany," said Holmes, as he took out his notebook and began to study the notices from the left side.

I began from the right side. "What exactly are we seeking?" I asked absently. No answer came. Only after he and I had read all the postings, did he respond.

"Did you read anything of interest, Watson?"

"Sorry Holmes, but nothing I read has aroused my suspicion."

The gleam in his eyes caused me to immediately regret my vapid remark. Holmes directed me to a re-reading of one posting.

Kathleen Ni Houlihan,

Meet me at the trolley and we'll rally in their arms.

Grace T. Rosemen

Rm 317

"The salutation is not that uncommon in this atmosphere of literary enlightenment. The name, 'Kathleen Ni Houlihan', has become an alias for Ireland, complements of a poem by the same name in the last century. Nonetheless, it focused my attention. The ambiguity of the trolley reference was also noted, but barely.

"Secondarily, Watson, I must digress to explain an interest which I have hitherto kept from you. Namely, my study of Irish surnames. Ireland has one of the oldest systems of heredity surnames.

"The signatory surname on the note in question is not a valid surname in Ireland. The name it resembles is 'Roseman', ending in *man*, not *men*. Actually, the surname, 'Roseman', is of German origin, having come to Ireland sometime in the 1600's.

"Quite naturally, I considered that the author of the note may have intended 'Rosemen' as a symbol for something German. This possibility alerted my instincts to a full alert and battle stations. I was reading a note to Ireland, from Germany, at a time when the latter was threatening war in Europe. Of the three nouns in the body of the note, only one, 'arms', was a clear reference to something military: 'rifles'; and we have been sent by the King to prevent rifles being landed here.

"My mind next centered on the name we were given by Declan O'Dempsey, as I was studying the signature name on the note. 'Roger Casement' versus 'Grace T. Rosemen'. Move the T to the end of Rosemen to get Rosement; which is similar to Casement. Swap the Ro for the Ca in Grace, and Rosement becomes Casement. You are then left with Grroe which can be rearranged to become Roger!

"Thus, 'Grace T. Rosemen' is an encoded version of 'Roger Casement'!

"When these clues had all congealed into the 'insight' I just described, the next clue in the note popped out at me. 'Trolley' was the destination of the arms shipment (i.e., Tralee (Bay)) in the west of Ireland.

"The phrase 'rally in their arms'; rather than two girls gathering in the arms of their boyfriends, comes to mean 'gathering in the rifles' from the ship landing them."

"Brilliant, Holmes!" I ejaculated, "Bravo!"

We retraced our steps to O'Connell Bridge, this time crossing over it into the heart of downtown Dublin. The telegraph office was located beside the General Post Office, just ahead on the left side of O'Connell Street.

Holmes sent the following telegram:

Friday
17 July 1914

Prime Minister Asquith:
Relate St. Patrick's Day event.
Declan T. O'Dempsey
12B48E 35CDAD67

Holmes used a positional encoding scheme used by the Holmes brothers for highly confidential messages to the highest levels of the English government. The recipient would depend on Mycroft Holmes to decipher a message so encoded.

The first word identifies location: 'Relate' represents 'Tralee'.

The second word, or phrase, identifies date: 'St. Patrick's Day' is 17 March.

The third word identifies the task at hand: 'event' means 'accomplished'.

The sender name, 'Declan O Dempsey' in this instance, is always an encoding template. It is used to decode the numeral-letter entries beneath it. There are fifteen letter positions in the sender name. The numeral-letter pattern directly under the sender name represents the actual name being transmitted in code.

The actual name code has fifteen slots, or positions, each designating a specific number from 1 to 9, zero, or a specific letter from A to F. Notice that the sender name also has fifteen letter positions.

The pattern of Arabic numerals and alphabet letters appearing under the sender name, contains the actual name (encoded) .

Thus, the sender number, '12B48E 35CDAD67', is decoded as follows: The 1 equals the contents of the first position in the sender name: a 'D' . The 2 equals the contents of the second position in the sender name: an 'E'. The B equals the contents of the twelveth position in the sender name: a 'P'

Notice that the spaces between first, middle, and last names are ignored (i.e., in the sender name).

Note: the tenth position is represented by '0' (unused in this instance).

Also, that positions 11 thru 16 are represented by the letter series A thru F. The 4 equals the contents of the fourth position in the sender name: an 'L'. The 8 equals the contents of the eighth position in the sender name: an 'O'. The E equals the contents of the fifteenth position in the sender name: a 'Y'

And so, we have '12B48E' decoded as 'Deploy'. While '35CDAD67' decodes into 'Casement'.

The Holmes telegram decodes into:

Tralee March 17 Completed
Deploy Casement

The sender name positional code:
Sender name: Declan T O Dempsey
Sender number: 12B48E 35CDAD67
Decoded msg: Deploy Casement

The Holmes telegram, as it came to be known at the seat of English government, passed by the vigilant eye of the Home Rule faction (which we knew had your man employed in the telegraph office), undetected.

A British gunboat was soon dispatched to blockade the entrance to Tralee Bay. The actual shipment of arms was deterred from being landed in the west of Ireland.

Meanwhile, myself and Holmes went on a walking tour of Dublin town for several hours. Passing by the Abbey Theatre, we stopped in. We had first passed by the Volta, on Mary Street, the first moving-picture house in Dublin.

A local schoolmaster, one Patrick Pearse, was conducting a rehearsal of a play he had written, in the Abbey. He was 'honored to meet the inimitable Sherlock Holmes' and welcomed us to attend his rehearsal. We spent there a pleasant interlude away from detection; although Holmes was more interested in the acoustics and the Georgian architecture of the domed ceiling.

We left Dublin City on the night ferry back to Holyhead, in Wales. We spent the night in the same hostel and departed for London in the morning of Saturday, 18 July.

Throughout the twenty-four hours of return travel we spoke at length on a subject which I will save for a rainy day.

Editor's Note:

Another British gunboat, which was sent to blockade Dublin Bay, was drawn away on a ruse concocted by the Home Rule faction. On Sunday, 26 July, a white yacht named Asgard came into Dublin Bay and docked at a quay in broad daylight. The Royal Irish Constabulary had been given the day off.

The Asgard, a 49 foot ketch, was loaded with 900 rifles and 29,000 rounds of ammunition. Hundreds of Irish Volunteers were on hand to receive rifles, minus the bullets. The boxes of ammunition were transported into Dublin in taxis.

Roger Casement, who had master-minded the gunrunning, was in Philadelphia awaiting a telegram informing of the result of the Asgard mission. His host was Joe McGarrity of the *Clan na Gael,* the leading Irish separatist movement in America.

End Note.

Holmes forever had mixed feelings regarding this adventure; considering it a half-success, half-failure. He believed we could have also prevented the landing at Dublin; had we not been ordered by the Crown to 'leave Ireland at once', upon their receiving the Holmes telegram. The King, himself, ordered the immediate return of Sherlock Holmes, an English lion in an Irish den, once the Tralee landing had been detected.

The Secret Adventure of the Great White Ape

Shall I continue, dear reader, in the vein of secret adventures by presenting perhaps the most personal tale ever participated in by my good friend and intimate associate? Dare I retell the untold account, after Holmes categorized created a new level of confidentiality, *inter nos,* to maintain its secrecy for five score and ten years? The force of Holmes' edict is with me, even though I record this story in my mind; believing as I do in Holmes' recently acquired knowledge of seers and mystics; believing that my mentally composed narration will exist somewhere in the great unconscious of humankind, inaccessible to all but the seer that comes along only once in each century.

I arrived at 221 Baker Street by Hansom cab in mid-morning of a blustery day in March, after escorting my wife to meet the morning train to the Midlands. In addition to my medical bag, I was carrying an overnight satchel containing the amenities for an extended visit with the world's greatest consulting detective, while Mrs. Watson was visiting with her relations in the country.

Holmes was leaning out one of his sitting room windows on the second story, his body facing skyward at a precarious angle with the horizontal, as I made my egress from the horse-drawn carriage, and went inside.

Unruffled by the levitation act, I stowed my bags and sat next the fire upstairs with a cup of tea from the pot on the rolling tray left my Mrs. Hudson. Holmes re-entered the room after dangling out near upside down.

"We're in for a northwester, Watson," said he.

"I packed accordingly, Holmes. The goodwife is gone for a fortnight to visit with her family in the Midlands."

"A Hindu maxim instructs married couples to 'Let there be spaces in your togetherness'," said Holmes with bright eyes.

Glad to see me he was; double goes for the prospect of amiable companionship during a ferocious nor'wester storm known to blow for two weeks this time of year. Holmes was subject to his black mood during this rite of spring in the British Isles. I planned to engage him in an attestation of our exploits together, with the secondary intent to gain his assent to my recording one or several adventures yet unrevealed. My primary intention was to fend off the black mood he was predisposed to experience.

"These scones are gustable!" said Holmes in a Scotch idiom. "Let us eat, drink and be merry." He was in high spirits.

"Yes, by all means, let us be joyful," said I, as I buttered a blueberry scone, one of Mrs. Hudson's finest. We made some small talk, or 'chatter', concerning the impending weather front and also regarding Mrs. Watson's train schedule. After brunch, Holmes began to whistle while he walked to the mantelpiece for a pipe. Never, in all our time together, had I heard Holmes whistle.

Throughout the afternoon, Holmes remained jubilant, monitoring a chemistry experiment, rummaging in his file cabinets, making entries in notebooks, putting turf on the fire, and playing his violin. I remained in my favorite armchair, near the fire, reading a penny novel about an American cowboy, with occasional pausing for a nap.

At tea time, Mrs. Hudson brought up a light supper of tea and sandwiches. Afterwards, I decided to broach the subject that had been vexing me.

"Tis bloody marvelous to see you in such an encouraging mindset," I remarked.

"Yes, Watson. I'm fit as a fiddle, as the saying proclaims. Haven't felt so well since my old school days."

"Perhaps we can enjoy a pleasant evening reminiscing of our adventures which remain unknown to the public. I have my notebooks with me," I countered cagily.

"I am in a most agreeable mood, my dear friend. Wind and weather permitting, I shall be your raconteur for the evening. Batten down the hatches, matey, for I've a tale to tell," he began.

While he carefully built up the turf fire in the fireplace, I retrieved a notebook from my bag in the spare bedroom.

"Your demeanor this day informs me that you have a mind to seek a special boon from me. Normally you would be happy to receive my blessing on any one of the unwritten adventures; but this evening you are after bigger game. You wish to learn my whereabouts during the hiatus in our relationship in the three years between May 6 1891 and April 1894."

"Once again, you astound me, Holmes," I replied, "but how on earth could you know?"

"It's elementary, Watson. The scale weight of your notebook-laden travel bag, amplified by the tones in your voice, augmented by your word choice in conversation, diminished by some minor cunning in your eyes, all harmonizing to reveal a quest to uncover my whereabouts during the Great Hiatus of purlieus Sherlock Holmes.

"Let us return to the year, 1891!

"I was contacted by a peerage family by the name of Greystoke. The father of one Lord Greystoke called here to implore me to find his son and daughter-in-law, Lord and Lady Greystoke, who had disappeared during a voyage to British West Africa. Lord Greystoke, John Clayton, had been appointed by the Colonial office to a new post. Lady Alice, his new wife, accompanied him. They arrived at Freetown in mid-June and wired a telegram home. Then they chartered a smaller sailing ship named, Fuwalda, to take them to the British West Coast African Colony. The Fuwalda has made no port of call since it left Freetown with the Claytons on board.

"In no time I was on board the next English warship that was headed for the region. The First Lord of the Admiralty, a friend, was a school chum of the senior Greystoke. The identity of the HMS naval vessel must remain *in pectore,* in order to avoid accusations of nepotism. Let us call it the HMS Peregrine as an alias. It resumed its normal patrolling off British West Africa, in the Atlantic, after debarking me at Freetown, Sierra Leone. Before my leaving the ship, the weather officer informed me that although the tropical depression season prevails during the summer months, there had been no storms off the coast in June.

"I booked into the hotel for foreign visitors as Fintan Mac Firbus, a natural history scientist from the British Museum. A few well-placed shillings later led me to the only trustworthy guide in this capital city of this backward country. As I had hoped, he had been hired by the Claytons, also; during their brief stay at the same hotel some weeks earlier.

"It took several days of reconnoitering the area, at a guinea a day, before I was whizzo in extracting whatever pertinent information about the Claytons this reliable guide might possess, albeit unknowingly. He was the go-between in their seeking a ship to rent. He cautioned them to decline any dealings with the captain of the Fuwalda, but they chose to ignore the advice; to their subsequent peril. For, given the good weather report, the nature of the captain, and the character of his ship, one is pressed to conclude that some sort of foul play had occurred.

"In August, the wreckage of the barkentine, Fuwalda, was found on the coast of St. Helen, by a British warship. Thus, my general analysis of their probable fate had come to pass, although it was not evident why the little ship had floundered absent stormy weather.

"Let us now jump forward ten years to the year 1901, with my expiation for leaving the three years of the Great Hiatus; but the tale directs it.

"British warships that patrol the Atlantic off the coast of British West Africa had recently discovered an island with a natural harbor, sitting about a week's sail out of Freetown. This previously unknown and uncharted island quickly became a fresh water stop for our ships returning to England. Returning seamen began telling of a tribe of huge apes seen on this unknown island; and of an albino ape among them. When these recountings reached the curator of The British Museum, he enlisted me to head an expedition to the island to observe this 'great white ape' – as he called it.

"I led the expedition to Simians Island, as it had been named, in June of 1901. We made anchor in the landlocked harbor in a small sailing vessel rented at Freetown. Unlike the foredoomed Lord and Lady Greystoke of a decade earlier, we brought our own crew.

"We made camp in a clearing, fifty yards behind the wooded shoreline, a waterside which was ringed in semi-tropical vegetation. The land all around rose to distant, lush hills. Birds were ubiquitous, along with small lizards and mammals. Fruit trees were abundant.

"At the edge of the glade, a small stream flowed into the cove. Traces of fruit-gathering by sailors were evident. The jungle sounds were cacophonous by day and concordant at night.

"On the second day, I made my way around this small bay by following a footway presumeably made by English seamen. One of the military hands always accompanied me during my jauntings on the island. Reports of the tribe of huge apes were fresh in our minds. That evening, we heard the ungodly roaring.

"On the third day, we saw the apes. A troop of manlike, hairy apes swinging through the treetops near the innermost shore, farthermost from the sea. That night they came to the edge of our camp, just across the stream, to drink and rest. There were several dozen of them. Astoundingly, one of the creatures appeared to be near-human!

"The next morning, I formulated a plan devised to catch the manlike albino ape. I supervised the construction of a cage of bamboo with a trap door entrance that could be dropped closed once the ape was inside. We placed the cage near their drinking place at the stream. A pile of fruit was set inside as bait. Lifting the pile allowed the entrance gate to fall down, springing the trap.

"During the night a loud melee erupted alongside the stream. Roaring and shrieking ensued along with the boom-crack of bamboo. We found the cage ripped asunder, apparently to free an entrapped ape.

"At daybreak, I had the men clean and check their rifles and strap on loaded bandoleers. We had no idea what a troop of enraged apes were capable of; but we knew they were extremely strong and most likely ferocious. We began standing a twenty-four hour guard.

"On the seventh night a full moon rose out of the primeval forest, atop the highest pike across the cove. My tent mate was on guard duty, patrolling the perimeter of our small camp. Thanks to his brilliant suggestion, I was sleeping with my right hand on my pistol, tucked under my pillow.

"I was dreaming of a visit to the London Zoo, when I was suddenly bounced awake as I was being hauled out of my tent and taken captive by a great ape and the albino ape-man! With the ape-man in the lead, and with me under the long arm of the great ape – like a rag doll – we were soon flying silently through the canopy, from vine to vine, like a circus performance.

"I still had my pistol. I had a chance to use it at first, before we were airborne, but my instincts did not place me in any danger, so I declined to shoot them. I considered firing a shot to scare them, but I did not want to be perceived as a threat.

"Soon after daybreak we descended into a glade. The great ape put me on the jungle floor, gently; confirming my initial, instinctual response. When my head cleared of dizziness, I looked up only to be stunned in amazement. The albino ape-man was a white boy!

"He dismissed the great ape with a hand gesture. He was sitting opposite me with a friendly expression on his youthful face and an eager glint in his blue eyes. We sat and stared at one another for awhile. Neither of us spoke. I took him to be a young teenager. His amazonian body build bespoke his trapezial skills. He rose and gestured for me to follow him to the foot of a huge solitary tree in the center of the clearing. When we reached the tree, he climbed up a vine and dropped down a rope ladder. I climbed up the bamboo rungs to a height of thirty feet, where he helped me onto a wooden platform about six feet square, perched on a huge fork in the massive tree. Wedged in the interior of this giant baobab tree, sat a cottage in the sky, hardly visible from ground level.

"To reach it, we crossed a rope and bamboo footbridge to an open porch that was on two sides of the log cabin. The window openings included a lattice of branches to prevent animal incursions. The heavy door was built of packing boxes and swung on wooden hinges. Once inside, a thick timber was the locking mechanism. Handmade furniture and implements occupied the room, including table and chairs, bed, washstand and shelves. The cabin was weatherproofed, roof and walls. The walls of three inch diameter sapling logs had been neatly chinked with a clay that must have been manufactured on site; probably five to ten years earlier. This estimate was based on the consistency, hardness, and brittleness of the mortar samples I examined.

"The dauber of these cabin walls was a member of the *homo sapiens* species!

"Meanwhile, the aboreal white gossoon had left me alone to go run an errand of some kind in the wilderness below.

"You who know me best, Watson, know of my tendency to be flippant whenever I am deeply moved. Recognize my referring to this lad as a 'gossoon' is actually a term of affection. After all, it was all too obvious to me that this cabin had been built by this boy's parents, some ten or twelve years prior, and they had perished before their son was a year old. I based this estimate on the boy's lack of human speech, and on his use of ape speech.

"Watson, this unfortunate urchin had been raised and suckled by these giant apes! Oblivious to my own imperilment, I was overcome by a desire to help this lost soul.

"As I awaited my companion's return, I noticed some stenciling on the inside of the door. It read:

"Some sort of cipher, was my first thought. Could it be hieroglyphics? The fourth and seventh symbols were the same; most likely a vowel. A closer look at a lower board on the door revealed the number '1', twice the height of the symbols. So I made the assumption that the symbols represented only half – the lower half – of their full representation. Then, substituting the first of the five vowels, (A, E, I, O, U), I produced:

"Extending the first and fifth symbols to a vertical conclusion, I had:

"The third symbol position was wider in spacing, so I tried a 'W':

"Of the four possibilities for the first symbol (B, F, P, or R), it must be an 'F'' because the horizontal line is straight.

"The second position cried out for a vowel, and only a 'U' or an elongated 'O' would fit. I liked the 'U'.

"The sixth symbol can only be the 'D' in 'Fuwalda', the name of the missing ship chartered by the Claytons out of Freetown in 1991, ten years ago!"

"By Jove, Holmes!" I bellowed, "You have fathomed the mystery of the Lord and Lady Greystoke's vanishing."

"Patience, Watson, there is more to relate. Permit me to continue.

"I had already deduced the essence of a sad tale of a couple of castaways, either shipwrecked or mutinously deposited onto this godforsaken archipelago. The man, intelligent, constructed the cabin; the woman, with child, proceeded to give birth to a boy; their subsequent demise and the infant's survival with the apes.

"I had ceased to remember the decade old account of the Greystoke incident, until the name, 'Fuwalda', triggered an instantaneous recollection. 'This aboreal superboy is the current Lord Greystoke?', I thought to myself, before falling into a deep sleep on the cabin floor in the treetop.

"When I awoke, he was sitting opposite me again, with a pile of fruit and some nuts and berries alongside. He then pushed some fruit towards me and made an eating gesture. As we ate, we tried to communicate; me in English, he in Ape.

"I was in a quandary unlike, and more perplexing, than any other predicament in my long career; for I could conceive of no practical solution to my dilemna.

"He had abducted me for some reason I was unable to discern. I was not able to make my way out of this paradox of my own accord. I was in reality a prisoner. 'This could very well be the end of Sherlock Holmes!', I thought.

"Despite my deep-set apprehension, I slept the night through. I woke to the cacophony of the ancient forest jungle. The magnificent boy-ape had slept on the floor, just inside the door. After a breakfast of banana and mango, we began a dialogue most unique in the history of civilizations. An educated man from Christendom attempting to confabulate with a boy raised as an ape; a lad whose ignorance of the essence of being human was nonpareil. Somehow, I had to bridge the gap between our mentalities.

"So, we began by trying to teach one another our respective language, His efforts to impart his words to me, I found extremely encouraging. Evidence of a rudimentary, innate intelligence; and a few books, leftover from the Claytons' time living in the cabin; were the touchstone of my educative success. After three months of intensive, daily instruction, my pupil had a child's working knowledge of the King's English! He knew the alphabet and could read, write, and speak simple sentences.

"When the time came for me to leave, he escorted me back to the vicinity of the small bay. We waited there until the next ship came into the harbor to load a fresh supply of water. I went to join them without my jungle friend, who waved to me before his ascent back into his homeland.

"Once aboard my rescue ship, I was not surprised by the friendly captain's revelation that since my 'disappearance' back in June, all His Majesty's ships sailing in these waters had been 'ordered' by the First Sea Lord of the Admiralty, himself, to make every concerted effort to locate me on this island, during scheduled port calls for water.

"As for how to explain my sojourn in the wilderness, I fabricated a tale that implicated no one but myself for my wandering away a summer on Simians Island."

Editor's Note:

Sherlock Holmes, until this disclosure to Dr. Watson, never spoke of his summer student on Simians Island. He believed that the jungle boy's continued happy existence demanded an absolute secrecy regarding anything pertaining to the lad. A sequestration that trumped the Greystoke family's prerogative to be informed of the existence of one of their own.

Another decade went by before another English ship, 'Arrow', landed a party of sailors who remained on Simians longer than the usual one or two days at anchor for fresh water. The civilians with the party, Professor Porter and his daughter, Jane, made contact with the ape-man; as described in Edgar Rice Burrough's book, 'Tarzan of the Apes'.

End Note.

The Secret Adventure of the Whitechapel Murders

I have elected to compose the following narration in my mind, seeing as how it involves the most heinous adventure Sherlock Holmes ever had the misfortune of encountering; this is the most confidential tale of all, to be stamped top secret until the 21st century.

"Whomsoever the psychic be who chances upon the encoding of this egregious episode," said Holmes to me during our discussion upon the wisdom of enumerating this narrative of penultimate evil, "residing out there in the Elysian Fields of historical events, where also resident are the *ne plus ultra* narratives, stored in the realm of the clairvoyants; pray tell, may this psychic honor my stipulation governing the transmission of this bizarre tale into the public domain."

On a foggy autumn day in London in 1888, Sherlock Holmes summoned me to return to Baker Street post haste. I was on a fishing holiday in Scotland at the time. After an overnight train trip from Aberdeen, I arrived in London the next morning.

Holmes was reclining on the sofa in the sitting room while reading a morning newspaper when I came in.

"There is a 'recurrent killer' operating in the East End, Watson," said Holmes from behind *The Globe*. "Why was your train twenty minutes late?"

"Just before entering the fog in the lowlands, the train was halted to allow the dispersal of a flock of sheep which was loitering on the tracks by the light of the moon," I replied.

"In the vicinity of Hadrian's Wall, I presume," said Holmes, "where the remains of the Roman Occupation are still evident."

As he stood up and went to the mantlepiece for a pipe, I noted the *Bradshaw Railway Guide* on the tea table and realized precisely how he knew I was twenty minutes late.

Pipe lit, he continued. "Digression can be of value even to the most ratiocinative mind, Watson. Akin to moving the main course to a rear burner of the stove, where it may simmer to fruition; while using the vacated front burner for one of the minor items of the meal in progress.

"As you have no doubt surmised, my friend, the reason for the premature ending of your rightful holiday is of consequence.

"A madman is slitting throats in the East End. I am expecting a message from Scotland Yard within the quarter-hour. Two women have been slaughtered in the month of August!"

"I must admit to feeling almost relieved to learn the nature of the emergency. When your telegram reached me, I was wading in a trout stream. The thought of a crisis nearer to home did cross my mind," said I.

"Like a good trooper, upon hearing the call of the regimental bugler, you rode to the sound of the guns. No more could be asked of any Englishman."

The front doorbell rang downstairs and Mrs. Hudson responded. After footsteps on the stairs, came a knock at our door.

"Come in, Sergeant," Holmes cried out.

And like a skit down at Lyceum, a sergeant of the Metropolitan Police entered.

"Good day, Mr. Sherlock Holmes. The Chief Inspector has sent me to escort you and Dr. Watson down to Scotland Yard."

"Very well, Sergeant. Give us a moment," replied Holmes.

"As you like, Mr. Holmes. I'll wait out front. I have a cab waiting," said the sergeant.

After the sergeant made his egress and we were preparing to depart, I looked at Holmes with a quizzical eye.

"How on earth did you know he was a sergeant?" I asked.

"All too easily, my dear Watson. Firstly, by the importance of the investigation. I expected to hear from the Chief Inspector, rather than from either Inspector Le Strade or Inspector Gregson. The Chief Inspector of the Metropolitan Police of London, England does not send a constable to represent him.

"Secondly, the measured knock on the front door, augmented by a disciplined footfall up the stairs, confirmed my presumption. And now, Watson, let us hasten to Scotland Yard."

The London four-wheeler waiting at the curb was one of the regulars which operated from Scotland Yard. The coachman nodded as we stepped up into the enclosed carriage, or growler. He drove us along Baker Street and on to Berkley Square, a side route he apparently preferred. When we arrived at and disembarked at the Yard, he drove his coach to the end of the queue of Hansoms and four-wheelers lined up along the long wall perimeter.

The Chief Inspector's office was on the main floor. He greeted us warmly and had us sit in his visitor chairs, across from his, behind a great oaken desk.

"So good of you both to come, gentlemen. We have a situation here. A deranged madman has butchered two 'Unfortunates' in the East End since the seventh of August. One more such incident and we may have full panic in the city; already, people are avoiding the streets in the evening.

"I have formed a task force and they are working around the clock to capture this fiend. Can you assist us?"

"As a self-appointed examiner of all criminal behavior, you shall have my comprehensive cooperation in this endeavor. May God help us!" said Holmes.

"Good man, Holmes. I thank you in the name of the King."

"Long live the King!" said Holmes and Watson, both standing.

The Chief Inspector also rose to his feet in acknowledgment of the king; a nine-hundred year old tradition in the realm of Britain.

The following day was a Saturday, September 8, 1888. I had office hours at my practice. Sherlock Holmes spent the day scurrying about the city of London, "The Square Mile", an area which was outside the jurisdiction of the Metropolitan Police. Like a mountain man checking his line of animal traps in the Rocky Mountains of America, Sherlock Holmes was seeking out the Agency, his network of snitches and petty thieves from whom he was able to glean information on criminal schemes and goings-on.

He also contacted the Baker Street Irregulars, his personal army of stipendiaries, to put them on the alert. They were directed to patrol the East End on an around-the-clock schedule, in pairs, with a bounty of ten pounds payable to the street urchin who is responsible for the capture of the killer, dead or alive.

Holmes and I returned to our flat at nearly seven that evening. Mrs. Hudson came up with our supper soon after. There were two tea cups on the salver. Holmes devoured his meal in a display of atavism uncharacteristic of him. It was only after a second cup of hot tea when we broke the silence.

"Watson," said he, sitting back in his armchair and steepling his fingers, "I have been analyzing all we learned at Scotland Yard yesterday pertaining to the two heinous murders in Whitechapel. Although it may deem impossible to discern a pattern of behavior from only two incidents, nevertheless I believe there is a likelihood of a third murder in the East End, to occur this portentous evening."

"Good heavens, Holmes," I said, "what have you perceived?"

Holmes got up and went to his bedroom to retrieve one of his favorite pipes from among those resident on the mantlepiece. He returned with the briar pipe already lit and stood beside the fireplace from which he often pontificated.

"Consider the dates of the two murders in August; the seventh and the thirty-first. The former occurring one week into the month; the latter on the last day of the month. The end of the first week and the end of the month. Take note that the seventh was a bank holiday and the thirty-first a Friday; a day off from work and the end of a work week.

"I'll grant you Watson, the weakness of this theory, but some degree of probability singles out tonight for another killing."

Next morning came a banging at the door of the flat. A voice in the hall was calling 'Mr. Sherlock Holmes'. I answered the door, wearing my new, lightweight, summer pajamas. A constable entered in a frenzy. Mrs. Hudson was only a few steps behind him with the early morning tea. She was one to arise with the warblers. The constable insisted upon conveying a message of the highest degree of urgency to the personage of Mr. Sherlock Holmes.

Whether or not Holmes had heard the bunctious arrival of the caller, I could not say with certainty at the time. Holmes preferred to rise of his own accord; besides, I was a bit miffed over my exclusion by a low-ranking constable.

"Constable," I said somewhat authoritatively, "you might as well sit and have a cup of tea. Mr. Sherlock Holmes, like the sun itself, rises when he rises."

"Very well, sir," he replied, "but something horrible has happened."

Right on cue, Holmes emanated from his bedroom to join the impromptu tea party. He had heard the commotion, as I had surmised.

Having gained his composure, the constable sat silently sipping his tea, waiting to be addressed by the Great Detective. Holmes selected his casebook and a folder from his filing cabinet before joining us.

"Good morning, Constable," said Holmes. "You have come to announce another Whitechapel murder, I presume."

"I have, your honor. Another 'Unfortunate' was found butchered only an hour ago."

Some of my good friend's thinking ability was beginning to rub off on me, I suppose, for I was able to fathom how he knew that a murder had occurred. So, I opted to remain silent rather than to utter one of my typical remarks of incredulity.

Holmes quickly dispatched the constable after listening to the gory details of his message. Rapidly, we dressed and rushed outside to hail a cab for Whitechapel.

Inspector Joseph Chandler of Scotland Yard was waiting for us to arrive. He was the inspector on duty when the body was discovered at approximately six o'clock in the morning, at 29 Hanbury in the East End.

The mortuary was a shed at the Whitechapel Workhouse. The East End had been without a proper mortuary since the old one had been demolished to make way for a new road.

The viewing of the body was a surrealistic experience far beyond the nightmarish encounters of any human being. I doubt the Mongol hordes of the thirteenth century ever committed the inhuman atrocities which were inflicted upon the living woman who was now reduced to the butchered remains on the table before us. Sherlock Holmes insisted it was unnecessary for both of us to experience the nightmare viewing; so I was spared the detailed examination of the corpse. I waited outside while Holmes and the inspector went over the cadaver.

When Holmes came outside a half-hour later his face was ashen grey and he was speechless. He first spoke in the cab while returning home, as we neared Baker Street.

"In all the annals of Western Civilization and Christendom..."

He left the sentence unfinished.

Despite having predicted the murder, Holmes was unable to relish the fruit of his ingenious deduction. His normal mode of behavior at this juncture in a case would have him alert and eager, like a bloodhound straining on the leash. Instead, he retired to his bedroom and a syringe of cocaine solution.

Holmes' theory now predicted an intermittence until the end of this month of September, when the next pogrom of unfortunate women in Whitechapel would resume. Thus, he had three weeks in which to find the proverbial needle in the haystack; in this plight, seeking out a homicidal maniac in a stockyard of despair.

The next three weeks were a whirl of social activities for myself and Miss Mary Morstan, whom I intended to marry, should she have me. Weekends, we were house guests at the country home of one of my wealthy patients; who had taken a patron-like interest in me, and an avuncular attentiveness to the winsome Miss Morstan. Weekdays, I had a backlog of scheduled appointments with patients during the day, and an affair of the heart each evening.

I would return home to Baker Street each evening before midnight. Holmes had taken to keeping late hours, prowling the streets orchestrating his minions in pursuit of the demonic killer. Each morning, when I arose, he would be sound asleep; occasionally his snoring could be heard in the living room. Mrs. Hudson was unable to stifle a giggle, nearly spilling the tea whenever she heard him sawing wood in the morning.

Editor's Note:

Prior to the advent of the Whitechapel murders, a stage production of Dr. Jekyll and Mr. Hyde opened at the Lyceum Theater in London and ran nightly during the time frame of the string of murders that became attributed to an unknown writer-of-letters sent to the Metropolitan Police; letters signed "Jack-the-Ripper".

A popular theory conjectured that the showing at the Lyceum was the catalyst that produced the chemical explosion in the brain of the killer; a reaction heretofore undocumented in the medical literature.
End Note.

September 28, 1888 was a Friday. Holmes had left me a note the evening prior, affixed to the entrance door of the flat with a stabbing knife. It read:

W.
Wake me for breakfast at 8.
The fiend is poised to strike again.
H.

We fell back into our morning breakfast ritual. The tea was hot and the scones were warm and all was right between us.

"Yes, Watson," said Holmes, having read my expression of contentment, "and all the ships are out to sea."

"You read my mind," I replied.

"I trust your courtship of Miss Mary Morstan is proceeding on course."

"Tis, Holmes, steady as she goes."

"Beware the rocks and shoals, my friend," said Holmes.

"A fine first mate will Mary be," said I continuing the language game.

"It takes a worthy mate to withstand a mutiny on board," said Holmes. "And tis the captain that checks the mate."

The reference to the chess move was a subtle signal to end the word game. After a wee pause, Holmes would reveal why he invited me to breakfast.

"Watson," he began after clearing his throat, "the Whitechapel killer will strike again tomorrow evening! I am certain of it. Sometime between sundown Saturday and dawn

Sunday, most likely. The pattern is clear; the last weekend of the month.

"Scotland Yard agrees with my analysis and will send squads of men to the East End beginning tonight--he could decide to kill this evening, one night early—to patrol from dusk to dawn.

"My Baker Street Irregulars have enlisted their older brothers, fathers, and uncles to join them, as per my orders, in four-man patrols. There will be two men and two boys in each patrol, armed with bats, clubs, and whistles. I have increased the reward to twenty-five pounds."

"Make that fifty pounds!" I interjected.

"Will you be available to accompany me tomorrow evening, Watson?"

"By all means, Holmes. I wouldn't hear of you going it alone."

"Bring your pistol. I will have my blackthorn shillelagh," he replied.

After spending a very pleasant Saturday with my new fiancé, I returned to Baker Street in order to have a working tea with my flatmate.

I found Holmes in a prone position on the Persian carpet by the bookcase. He was studying the map of the City of London which was opened flat on the carpeted floor.

"What's this, Holmes?" I remarked. "Are you contemplating a plan?"

He held his left index finger up to shush me and went on with his inspection of the outstretched map. Alongside were several vellum tracings apparently done by Holmes this day. On his right was a Geometry book and some drawing instruments.

At four o'clock, Mrs. Hudson came in with the tea and sandwiches as was our custom. She greeted me in a whisper, after seeing Holmes at work on the carpet, and tiptoed out.

As I was biting into a second, small sandwich, Holmes sprang to his feet to exclaim: "Euclidean Geometry is magnificent, Watson!"

"Precisely, Holmes!" I replied, unconsciously mimicking my illustrious partner. "Why, I can recall studying geometry in my school days at..."

"No matter, my dear friend," he interrupted, "we have a grave situation to address. Geometry provides us with axioms and theorems that can be useful in the ongoing, never-ending struggle between good and evil. Can you think of an application, Watson?"

"Offhand, I can't think of one," I answered.

"Firstly, we have three murders to date. Thus, logic suggests the geometric principle of the triangle. Come here, Watson! I have everything pertinent located on the map."

I went over to him and we knelt side-by-side at the bottom edge of the London map. Holmes had a pointer to touch areas and locations within the map without disturbing or wrinkling the horizontal plane it made with the floor.

"As you can now observe, I have drawn a triangle using the three red pins to mark the corner points. The base of this isosceles triangle runs along Commercial Street. The left side lies along Hanbury Street; the right side along Whitechapel Road."

Next, as I watched in captivation, Holmes used a protractor, straight edge, and a dividing compass - instruments used by engineering draftsmen - to divide each angle in half; laying down construction lines on the tracing, using a hard lead pencil which left light, thin lines on the transparency. He extended the three mid-angle lines until they intersected within the triangle. This intersect point he marked with a green locator pin. It fell on the intersection of Brick Lane and Fashion Street, on the underlying map of London. Next, using a soft lead pencil which left dark lines, he traced in the layout of the city streets that fell within the isosceles triangle.

Only when he paused to admire his work, did I interweave a question within his concentration.

"What is the significance of the green pin?" I asked.

"It locates the mid-point of the triangle, which marks the mid-point of the three murder locations. Thus, it has some significance to the mind of the killer. Perhaps marking the area, he is departing from each time he sets out to kill."

"I take it to mean that you think he lives in the vicinity of the green locator pin," said I.

"Perhaps, Watson. But I am more inclined to think that he lives elsewhere; each time coming into Whitechapel to murder one of London's Unfortunates; maybe operating from a rented premises, where he can discard his blood-spattered clothing after each killing. An obscure rental down a dark lane or mews, where he can retreat to after he strikes; in order to remove his bloody disguise, sleep until morning, and to reappear dressed as a gentleman out for a stroll through the East End."

After dark we hailed a Hansom cab which delivered us to the corner of Commercial and Wentworth streets, which spot was midway along the base of the triangle on the overlay sketch map in Holmes' possession. We walked up Wentworth to Brick Lane and turned to the left. After passing two streets on the left side, Thrawl Street and Flower & Dean Street, we came to Fashion Street, also on the left side of Brick Lane. We were at the geometric center of the killing ground.

On the opposite side of Brick Lane were warehouses, slum dwellings, and small, dark lanes leading to tenement sweat shops and dismal, dross houses. There were also some lofts and studios and garrets used mainly by poor bohemians. One group of four Baker Street Irregulars appeared suddenly out of shadows across Brick Lane and called out to us. Holmes sent them back into the warren of mendacity with a hand gesture. A light fog began rolling in from off the Thames.

We were standing under a gaslit street lamp on the corner. Holmes pulled out the tracing map from his inside pocket. As we were reading the sketch map we heard footsteps along Fashion Street. It was a constable walking his beat.

"Good evening, Mr. Holmes," the constable called out. He was one of dozens walking a beat in the East End this night.

"Good evening, Constable," said Holmes. "Carry on, but be wary. The fiend will strike again tonight!"

The usual bustle of people walking to and from public houses, including the many women of the night, was reduced to a trickle of humanity. Among the few foolhardy souls was a well-known artist, Walter Richard Sickert, and his model for the evening. He exchanged greetings with Holmes in passing.

Ten minutes after his first appearance, the constable passed by once more. No premises in Whitechapel would be outside the scrutiny of a passing constable for longer than ten minutes this evening.

From a distant church bell tower came ten bongs resonating throughout the dim, dark, dank ways and byways of the dreariest section of London.

"Come along, Watson, we have two hours to idle away. Our killer won't act till past midnight. We will walk this route which I have marked in a line of dashes on my tracing map. At each pub we pass we shall commingle with the sisterhood of streetwalkers still loitering there, oblivious to the dastardly demon determined to destroy them."

Holmes was speaking alliteratively, as he was apt to do whenever the concretion of determination came over him.

"What shall we say to the poor Unfortunates?" I asked.

"Let us tell those who reject our forewarning, to make peace with their maker, for one of their cortege tonight will surely butcher one from among their cohort of concubines."

We set off to walk the area bounded by Fashion Street on the north, Wentworth Street on the south, Brick Lane to the east, and Commercial Street to the west; an area nearly forming a square. Two cross streets ran between Brick and Commercial, inside the square; Thrawl Street and Flower & Dean Street.

"Holmes, how do you know the killer won't strike before midnight?"

"By the timing of the three murders to date: the first shortly after midnight; the second after half-two; and the third after half-five. He is trying to be unpredictable but he has always struck after midnight. He has gone through the six hours of darkness after midnight, one time, for three murders. Tonight he will most likely revert back to the first hour; sometime between midnight and one o'clock."

We spent the next two hours admonishing all we encountered to be off the streets by midnight. The bawdy scenes we grappled with in several public houses cannot be discussed in polite company; situations where the clientele were either indisposed or disposed to ignore us. Come midnight we were on station at the corner of Brick Lane and Fashion Street, the geometric center of Holmes' triangle of killing sites.

Editor's Note:

Sherlock Holmes prediction was doubly accurate, for on the night of Saturday, September 29, 1888, two gruesome murders occurred during the early morning hours of the Sunday; one at 0045 hours, the other at 0130 hours.

The first victim was found in Berner Street, Whitechapel, barely outside the perimeter of the Holmes triangle, with her throat cut and body mutilated. The second victim was found in Mitre Square, Aldgate, also just outside the Holmes triangle, also with her throat cut and body mutilated.

Dinsome mobs of neighborhood residents quickly formed at each murder scene making it impossible for Sherlock Holmes to employ his inimitable talents of detection.

End Note.

Several days passed during which we were involved in the aftermath of the night of the double murders. All the usual chores of investigating had our undivided attention. Leads were followed and suspects identified. Scotland Yard had two hundred men assigned to the case. We had been to the murder scenes on the Monday, after all the evidence had been washed away; Holmes said it was necessary in all cases to visit the scene of a crime, however late.

There were no more murders, of the sadistic slashing type, during the month of October, 1888. However, a string of letters purportedly signed, "Jack the Ripper" were mailed to the authorities and to the newspapers. Some were thought to be bogus, but some were obviously from the recurrent killer, who was henceforth called "Jack the Ripper". Apparently the letter-writing sublimated the sadistic pathology of the killer during the month of October.

It was Thursday, November 8, 1888. After breakfast we began chatting about the Whitechapel Murders.

"I awoke this morning with a vague premonition concerning the recurrent killer," said Holmes.

"Indeed. I suspect we have seen the last of him."

"Wishful thinking is the opiate of the unenlightened, my friend," said Holmes. "Remember the timing pattern of the killings. One week into the month, on a weekend; and the last day of the month. Despite the respite last month, my instincts are advising me to be vigilant this month."

"By all means do I defer to your judgement, Holmes, however you may have reached it," I replied.

With that said, Holmes finished his tea and went over to the mantlepiece for a pipe. I settled back in my easy chair to read the morning paper.

Our mid-morning pastime was intruded upon by a ruckus downstairs in the entrance hall. Mrs. Hudson was straining her English upbringing in her encounter with what can only be called, "a woman of the evening"; or, in the local vernacular, an "Unfortunate".

Holmes went downstairs, hushed the combatants, and returned upstairs with the Unfortunate woman in tow.

"Dr. John Watson," said Holmes upon entering our inner sanctum, "may I present Miss Mary Jane Kelly!"

"How do you do?" I responded formally.

"Pleased to make yer acquaintance, yer Lordship," she replied.

Holmes was tickled by the unfolding charade which was becoming worthy of Gilbert and Sullivan.

"Miss Kelly, kindly be seated and inform us of the purpose of your visit," said Holmes, suppressing a grin.

"T'ank you, Mr. Shoylock Holmes. O'im come here in daspiration consoinen' a mather of life and death. And tis me own life O'im tryin ta save!" said she, as she sat down.

"Why is your life in danger?" I asked.

"Tis the Whitechapel Murdhurer what wants ter moider me."

Holmes resorted to speaking to her in a soft, low voice. "Who is this murderer, Miss Kelly?"

"He's the man what wants ter kill me. Like he done dem other girrls."

"What is his name?" Holmes asked sharply, trying to jolt the girl into focusing her thoughts.

"His name is Jack-the-Ripper, Mr. Holmes!"

"Can you tell us, in your own words, the whole story? Start with where you live and work, and how you came to know this man," said Holmes.

"O'i can!" she replied. "O'i been stayin at number 26 Dorset Street. O'im from Oireland, ya see. Limerick. O'im a foine and daycent girrl when O'im sober, Mr. Shoylock; tis a different ting when O'ive had to dhrink.

"Moy man is one Joseph Barnett, a good man he is. Too good fer the likes of me, ya see.

"Ten Bells Public House in Commercial Street is me local pub, and a foine pub it tis. O'im an artist by thraining in Dublin ya see. O'im a sketch artist down at the pub, now.

"O'i like to dhraw humorous sketches of the customers down at the pub. Of the regular customers, in particular. Whenever O'i ament able ta sell a sketch, O'i takes it home wit me. Sure an dere's a dhrawer full of them, until raysently anyway.

"O'i'll tell ya somethin fer nuthin, Mr. Shoylock. Doze foive murdhers what took place in Whitechapel, I knew all foive a doze girrls, poor Unfortuates dey was. Tis because of me dey was killed!"

After pausing for a drink of water, she continued.

"Acktrickly, it were the sketches what got dem killed. Jack the Ripper, as dey named him in the newspapers, tinks dat I must'ave dhrawn him when he was in the Ten Bells Pub one avenin."

"Have you been questioned by either the Metropolitan Police or the City Police?" Holmes asked.

"O'i have!" she answered.

"Have you spoken of the sketches to them?"

"O'i have!"

"Did they show any interest in your sketches?"

"Dey only gave dem a wee glance."

"Why do you think your sketches are important to this case?"

"Because of the man with the black bag."

"The police are looking for the man with the black bag. What do you know of him?"

"O'i know that he ripped up the sketch of himself that O'i dhrew of him in the pub."

"When did this take place?"

"Twas a lovely avenin of summer just past."

"Did you mention this to the police?"

"O'i did not!"

"Why not?"

"Because no one spoke of the black bag."

"When did you come to know the police were looking for a man with a black bag?"

"On the Monday last. It were in the Sunday paper."

"This man that ripped up your sketch, would you be able to recognize him?"

"O'i would! Faces are my profession, when O'i ammint tipsy with the dhrink."

"How well did you know the five women who were murdered by the Whitechapel killer?"

"O'i knew dem from the pubs and the streets we all walked."

"Miss Kelly, I believe you very well may be the primary target of this vicious madman," said Holmes. "Your personal safety demands immediate action. So, you shall be under my protection and supervision until the killer is apprehended. Do you so agree?"

"O'i do, Mr. Shoylock, O'i surely do."

"A wise choice, Miss Kelly. We shall have hidden you at a safe location out in the English countryside before nightfall. Dr. Watson will make all the arrangements."

When I deposited Miss Mary Jane Kelly of Limerick City in the county of Clare, Ireland, in the four o'clock train for the west of England, she could have been mistaken for a genteel English woman returning home after a shopping excursion to London.

My good fiancé, Mary, had been responsible for this wonder-work. Miss Kelly had been transformed back into the beautiful young woman she was when she first came to England. Long black, conditioned, shoulder-length hair contrasted by a freshly- scrubbed alabastrine complexion and eyes of sparkling, tinker blue. She wore a long and proper dress in evergreen taffeta with a matching parasol. Stylish shoes supported the lines of an Irish filly thoroughbred descended from the original settlers of the magical isle to the west of England.

I waved to Mary from the platform as the train departed the station. Thence I hired a Hansom to take me to Baker Street. Her last words to me were in the Irish Gaelige. "*Dia dhuit*!"

I found Holmes down on the Persian carpet once again, working with his tracings and the map of London.

"Miss Kelly is safe and sound aboard the Midlands train!" I greeted Holmes.

"Excellent, Watson. Come and look at this."

I sat cross-legged to his right at ninety degrees.

"Take note of my first triangle tracing, Watson, which is pinned in place atop the city map. I have plotted the first two sites of the double murders of September 30th. Next I drew a line connecting these two murder scenes; it runs east-to-west along the orientation of the underlying map. It lies a bit outside the triangle.

"Now observe as I plot the location of Mary Kelly's room in Cooley's Lodging House at number 26 Dorset Street. Next I draw a light line from there to murder scene number four; and the same to murder scene number five. We have a new equilateral triangle, similar in size to the first isosceles triangle; but offset to the south and west.

"I see that Mary Kelly's location is a bit to the west of the base of triangle number one. So I find the mid-point of the base of triangle number one, using my divider compass, and lay in a light construction line from this midpoint to the apex of its triangle; which effectively bisects triangle number one.

"The points of triangle number one are sequentially numbered according to the consecution of the murder victims found thereunder. The two latest killing scenes have been numbered four and five, respectively, to represent the fourth and fifth victims of the recurrent killer.

"If my geometrical theorem formulated to decipher this case has any validity, then the following postulate will be meaningful: namely, that a second triangle, defined by points three, four and five will be necessary for a solution.

"Notice that this second triangle is an equilateral triangle! Also note that point one falls within the central area of this second triangle. Could point one be the geometric center of triangle two?

"I used the divider compass on this next overlay to bisect each angle in triangle number two. Eureka, Watson, a construction line that bisects angle three intersects point one; logically connecting the two triangles, consistent with the law of probability but not immune to the petty foggery of lawmongers.

"Gadzooks, Watson, the base line of triangle one is the line in triangle two that runs from the center of triangle two to the middle of angle three, in triangle two. The ingenuity of this relationship of triangles is exceptional.

"Doubting Thomases kindly take notice; the construction lines representing the bisection of each angle in triangle number two meet at point one in triangle number one! Q.E.D.!"

I was astonished, not only by the brilliance of Holmes' proof of his own theorem, but also by my comprehension of his presentation, so far, which was about fifty percent.

"I say, Holmes, this beats all!" I was able to comment. "This could be the touchstone case of your career. A most remarkable, awe-inspiring analysis."

"Thank you, Watson," he replied humbly. "Although I must insist upon classifying this adventure as another one for the time capsule."

"I concur completely, Holmes. It will take a century to attenuate the horror of these murders, if such atrocities can ever be diminished."

I began to stand up but Holmes motioned me with a raised hand to remain in place.

"Miss Mary Jane Kelly and her perception of persecution may serve as an acid test for my theorem; or, conversely the theorem may relegate her fears to the domain of paranoia. So, let us take a closer look at a point on the overlay marking the location of Miss Kelly's room in Dorset Street. It lies on the line from Point three, in both triangles, to point five in triangle two.

"Attention, Watson, to point six on this overlay of our two overlapping triangles! Can you see any method of linking it with triangle one, logically?"

"I am unable to think ahead regarding your geometry, Holmes, as I am struggling to understand it fully."

"Fair enough, my friend. It took me some time to develop the theorem. The *coup de grace* to confusion is the light of insight.

"Permit me to point out the definitive detail *vis-a-vis* Miss Kelly. The construction line that bisects triangle one, when extended, intersects point six! Ergo, Mary Kelly is the killer's next intended victim!"

"By God, Holmes, I see it!" I nearly shouted out as I rose brusquely to my feet. "The logical construction that ties the isosceles triangle to the equilateral triangle. It also extends to Mary Kelly."

Holmes got up from the carpet to join me in our usual chairs. The pain in my leg from floor-sitting had brought about a state of discomposure, during which I experienced a mental reliving of my wounding in Afghanistan. My perspicacious friend quickly poured me a snifter of Napoleon brandy. Only when I had regained my homeostasis did he resume his discourse.

"The extrapolation of criminal behavior in our time has its roots in Euclidean Geometry. While the latter is founded on the precepts of logic.

"The Whitechapel Murderer, also become known as Jack the Ripper, undoubtedly has a university education. He almost certainly is a professional in one of three fields of study: mathematics, art or drafting. An additional knowledge of medicine, including surgery, may also be involved," said Holmes, with a ten-fingered cupola on his thorax, sitting back in his easy chair.

"An amazing deduction, Holmes!" I replied in flabbergastation.

Holmes went to the mantlepiece to load his cherry wood pipe with Ship's tobacco. Soon his exhalations diffused into the ambrosial traces rising from my brandy, confederates in confronting clever criminals.

"We do have a situation, Watson. What will the killer do tonight, when he is unable to locate Mary Kelly, whom he has been stalking, I believe?" said Holmes.

"Stalking?" was my response. "Why did he not kill her sooner?"

"There is a question of greater significance to be asked, Watson. Is Mary Kelly the final point in the killer's geometry? Or, is she to be the first point in the third triangle?"

"Good Lord, Holmes! How many types of triangles are there?"

"Too many, Watson. We must end this madness tonight."

I arrived at the entrance to Miller's Court in Dorsett Street at eleven o'clock, after a pleasant evening spent with my fiancé, Mary. Holmes was waiting there for me. He had spent the evening marshaling the Baker Street Irregulars, junior and senior divisions, his infantry forces in the ongoing war with crime. They had been disbursed to stand guard at regular intervals the length of Dorsett Street from Crisp Street to Commercial. One group of four was stationed just outside Miller's Court. Holmes and I would patrol inside the courtyard. All had been alerted to be all eyes and ears from midnight till dawn.

People came and went all night, participants in a typical evensong of drunken debauchery in Whitechapel. At break of day Holmes dismissed his troops and we caught a cab home.

At two o'clock in the afternoon a telegram arrived from Scotland Yard. A woman's body had been discovered at 26 Dorsett Street in Mary Kelly's bed!

The severely mutilated body was identified (mistakenly) as Mary Jane Kelly by the coroner of London. In reality it was one of London's Unfortunates who will remain unknown. Jack the Ripper had claimed his final victim.

Mary Jane Kelly actually went home to Ireland and vanished into oblivion.

Editor's Note:

The Public Records Office has some two hundred odd letters on file from Jack the Ripper. One of these letters is signed:

"Yours truly, Mathematicus"

Jack the ripper was never identified!

End Note.

The Secret Adventure of the Regimental Bugle Boy

During the Great War, "the war to end all wars", it became necessary to prioritize the demands made upon "the world's greatest detective". The King and the Government began classifying their claims on Sherlock Holmes as either secret, top secret, most secret, or utmost secrecy. The last designation reserved for the King's use only.

Holmes relied upon myself to arrange multiple requests within category into chronological order. In my absence he would inevitably use a random shuffle technique; his offering to the gods of statistics.

The tale I am about to relate occurred during the sacrificial lunacy which was taking place in the fields of France. But due to it's low priority in the war scheme, Holmes and I were unable to take on this case until after the Armistice.

Early in February of 1919 Holmes had only returned from Germany on a mission involving allied prisoners of war. It had been over thirty-five years since our first adventure. We were both war weary and had taken to sleeping later in the morning. I still was able to sleep soundly despite the nightly bombings of London, where I spent the war. Holmes had made trips to the war zones of Europe on behalf of King and Country, which left him with recurring nightmares.

Mrs. Hudson had perished in the blitz; her daughter, Rebecca, had replaced her in our life at 221 Baker Street. So, it was now Miss Hudson what looked after "her two old uncles", as she called us.

The Tuesday morning it was. By half-nine I had consumed my scones and several cups of tea and was engrossed in the morning newspapers when Mr. Sherlock Holmes made an appearance.

"It's time we tackle the backlog, Watson," the voice preceding the man into the living room. In his sixty-fifth year, he was still able to project a commanding presence when entering a room.

"Good morning, Holmes," I replied ebulliently. "Top of the morning my Irish friend!" He had been gone the month of January.

His face answered me with his characteristic wee grin.

"Watson, old boy," he replied with a twinkle in his eyes, "if you must address me in the Irish idiom, kindly use the idiom of Ireland rather than the idiom of Irish America."

He paused in expectation after his linguistic gauntlet. As was my wont, I rose to the bait, like some speckled trout from its dimpled diggings.

"The *patois* English spoken in Ireland is not unknown to me, Holmes."

"'*Thar cinn'* in the Gaelic Irish translates, 'over the top'" he replied in the patient manner of a grade school teacher. "It has been corrupted in translation by the Irish American diaspora to 'top of the morning'."

Lacking a rejoinder, I ended the repartee with the following lame response: "What was it you said about a backlog, Holmes?"

Holmes had begun eating a blueberry scone after his last remark, anticipating my failure to continue in the lively give and take in which he excelled. He finished his tea and scone and sat back in his easy chair before answering.

"Watson, dear fellow, would you mind looking in the file for the cases which we placed in abeyancy until war's end. The folder concerning the British Army in Nigeria has bubbled up into my consciousness."

I located the file, and returned to my chair with the folder in hand. The lone letter inside read as follows:

Highland Regiment
Northern Nigeria
Summer of 1917

To whom it may concern:

This letter is being written to document for the record, the peculiar happenings which have occurred here during our suppression of the local tribal conflicts and uprisings.

We the British Army have had little trouble defeating spear-hurling natives. Their primitive weapons are no match for our riflery. Our casualties have been few.

Having put down all resistance, we have been serving as military overlords presiding over the local tribal chiefs and clan kings. The tribes throughout the region persist in their age old practice of slavery, mainly by the victors enslaving those whom they defeat in warfare. Harmony with the slave culture is required on our part in order to maintain the order necessary to control the tribes. Allowing the tribal leaders to rule in their own traditional fashion has resulted in their utmost cooperation with our regimental officers. We are simply not in a position to emancipate those natives here held in bondage.

The dominant tribe in Northern Nigeria is the Tiv. They practice a type of quasi-religion called "Akombo", which is supervised by a group of tribal Elders. They conduct secret ceremonies at night which we have been unable to decipher.

One alarming scenario which we have noticed is most aberrant. After each meeting of the tribal elders in the hut used solely as a meeting house for their "religion", one of the youth of the tribe's slave population goes missing. We are reluctant to speculate on these ramifications; but we fear the worst.

We feel obligated and duty bound to cast the light of civilization on this tribe and its heinous culture.

Col. Wendall McLaren
Commanding

"Why, this letter is nearly two years old!" I stated.

"Indeed, Watson. The time has come to look into the situation in Nigeria."

"What do you propose to do?" I asked dubiously.

"Rest assured, my friend, there will be no trip to British West Africa regarding this bizarre kettle of fish. Rather, I am inclined to begin this case by a meeting with the letter writer."

Next morning, the Wednesday, a hansom cab pulled up at ten o'clock sharp. A tall man disembarked and strode to the front door with a military bearing.

Miss Hudson granted him entry and led him upstairs. She knocked before announcing his arrival.

"Mr. Holmes, Colonel Wendall McLaren, responding to your telegram of last evening." Preceding him into the flat she placed the telegram on the entrance table and stepped aside for the guest to enter. She took his overcoat and left.

"Colonel McLaren, do come in," said Holmes. "This is my associate, Dr. Watson."

"Pleased to meet you both," replied the colonel, as he sat in the guest chair offered.

We resumed our chairs across the tea table from our visitor. Holmes opened a folder and silently read the colonel's letter written from Nigeria in 1917. In the interim, I offered a cup of tea to our prompt caller.

"Forgive me Colonel, for this tardy response to your Nigeria letter." Holmes finally spoke. "The bloody war, you know."

"Indeed," came the colonel's reply, followed by a tit-for-tat quietude.

We three enjoyed several sips of warm tea before Holmes spoke again.

"Good Colonel, can you expound on your letter?"

The square-jawed guest put down his tea cup and sat up ramrod-like in his chair. Worry and fear flashed in his blue-grey eyes and across his facial expression. He was apparently experiencing a memory flashback of, or concerning, his documentation of his regiment's service in West Africa.

"I can, Mr. Holmes, and I shall!" replied the colonel. "As you no doubt concluded when I mailed you a carbon copy of my letter, without designating you as a recipient; there was more to the situation in West Africa than I was willing to put down on paper."

"Indeed," replied Holmes, mimicking the good colonel's previous utterance. I was able to curb a grin in order to avoid being chagrined at Holmes' cheekiness. My associate had developed an impudent sense of humor in his greying years.

Holmes' verbal ploy went unrecognized by the colonel, who was absorbed in his own disturbing thoughts.

This time the colonel broke the silence.

"Mr. Holmes; Dr. Watson; what I am about to tell you may find you unwilling to believe. Nevertheless, tell you I must. The honor of my regiment and the structure of our civilization require no less.

"We went ashore in British West Africa in the summer before last, June 1917. The dominant tribe called themselves the Tiv. Under the British policy of 'indirect rule' the tribal leaders ruled over their subjects in much the same fashion as they did before English domination. The chiefs, themselves, however, had been forced to recognize the authority of their English overlords. Their allegiance to the Governor General and his ruling council was necessary to effect the subsumption of the tribal populace into the British scheme of things. This tenuous and sometimes fragile arrangement of control over the natives, the concept known as 'indirect control', has been relatively successful, allowing for imperial rule of some millions of natives by some few British troops in country.

"By design, this chain of command permits the ancestral daily life of tribal members to continue unabated. Chiefs and tribal elders are also left to conduct the traditions and business of their tribe, which includes the management of slaves captured in tribal wars. A leading indicator of a chief's wealth is the number of slaves he owns."

Sherlock Holmes, aided by a deliberate cough, interrupted with an asking.

"Has the British presence reduced the frequency and intensity of tribal warfare in all four of our colonies in West Africa?"

After a nervous cough, the colonel responded.

"It has been very difficult bringing down the level of violence in Nigeria; never mind the other colonies. The Tiv tribe have been most difficult. As I mentioned in my letter, they practice a bizarre religious practice that results in the disappearance of a young slave. Rumors of human sacrifice are ubiquitous; although one hopes for the best. Namely that the young slave has been sold to a neighboring tribe."

Another pause afforded Holmes to jump in again.

"Were you able to gather any evidence to support either outcome?" asked Holmes, leaning in toward the colonel.

"None whatsoever, Mr. Holmes. The jungle swallows up everything and digests it, as if it never existed."

At this point, Holmes looked to me for any assistance I might have to offer. The recondite deductionist seeking the practical observation of the mundane medicalist.

"The heinous practice of inter-tribal slavery, augmented by sales to ship captains bound for the Americas," I began pontifically, "led to the British Navy capturing 1287 slave ships off West Africa during the forty year period, 1825 through 1865. The 130,000 slaves on board these ships were dropped off on Sierra Leone as freed men."

"Indeed, Watson," remarked Holmes in a complimentary tone.

"Yes, Dr. Watson," began the colonel, "your facts are accurate, but what is not widely known is the undeniable reality that many of these rescued slaves were re-enslaved by the same tribal leaders who had first enslaved them.

"The custom has continued unabated these past fifty odd years. Africa is truly a dark continent."

"I say, Colonel McLaren," snapped Holmes rising to his feet, "what is it you are reluctant to reveal to us?"

"You are very perceptive, Mr. Holmes," the colonel replied with a sense of resignation. I must apologize for my timidity and henceforth speak more candidly concerning the matter that has haunted me for nearly two years. May I see the letter I sent to you, to refresh my memory?"

Holmes passed the letter to the colonel.

"Ah, yes," began the colonel. "My letter is more direct and to the point than myself speaking. My trepidation bubbles to the top of my consciousness at the reading on the page of the word, 'akombo', in all its malevolence.

"The belief system of the Tiv tribe which reeks of evil, lies beyond the understanding of the European mind. It is a soulless rite practiced in secrecy by simple-minded savages who are steeped in superstition. It is scapegoating used in the ancient form to assuage tribal suffering by casting blame on a selected victim. The victim is always a male slave youth, who subsequently vanishes. But, so long as this barbarism had no direct effect on any British citizens serving in Africa, the policy of 'indirect rule' remained sacrosanct.

"The unexplained disappearance of the Governor General's houseboy, a local native youth who had been enslaved by his tribe, before being rescued into a benevolent serfdom in the governor's residence, failed to provoke any official reaction or retaliation.

"It took the vanishment of the regimental bugle boy to rouse the British Lion. The dastardly deed occurred shortly after a severe acrimony had taken place between the tribal chiefs and the Governor's Council, involving the conduct of

British troops. Faced with such insolence, the governor issued a 'shoot when provoked' proclamation to the British soldiers. The tribal chiefs were informed of their susceptibility to the new policy.

"A short time later, the regimental bugle boy was reported as missing in action and presumed dead. Neither the regimental records nor the official war office records contain any mention of the suspicions held in the certain death of the bugle boy."

"What if the bugle boy has been sold into slavery?" I asked. "This is a possibility in your own words."

"Moreso in the case of a native slave easily assimilated into a native tribe, than in the case of a white youth whose existence would soon be conveyed over the native drum plexus. Thus certain to be learned of by those who serve the British interests in West Africa," the colonel replied.

Holmes had gone over to the mantlepiece to find a pipe and was enjoying the first puffs.

"Native drums are superior to our modern telegraph network," began Holmes, "lacking as they do the need to install wire-carrying poles for the length of the distance to the message receiver."

This verbal digression by Homes was symptomatic of a trait he developed in his middle years. It had become his way of winding down a conversation that had ceased to command his interest. Whereas in his younger years, he was inclined to be abrupt, and a bit rude, perhaps; he had decided later in life to be more attentive to the feelings of others.

And so, in short order, Holmes dismissed the colonel with assurances of Holmesian vigilance and follow-up. Only when the colonel's cab had been trotted off, did I turn to Holmes with a bone of contention.

"By God, Holmes!" I began, "What were you thinking? You sent the colonel packing, however politely, without hearing him out in full."

"Rest assured, Watson. The colonel told us all he was able to; all that his conscience would permit. An officer in the

British Army does not divulge secrets easily, pertaining as they do to his own regiment. The arcanum he is withholding has been stored in his memory with emotional wrappings. It cannot be released except in a torrent of emotion. This brave and decorated officer deserved the better treatment in our hands."

"Bloody marvelous touch on your part," I replied, a bit stunned by my friend's sagacity, which apparently knew no bounds.

After agreeing to return by tea time, we set off on separate missions of research; Holmes to the London Library to see about the Tiv tribe, while I set out for the Military History museum.

By four o'clock we were back in the bosom of 221 Baker Street and a warm fire in time for tea. Afterwards we examined one another's findings and decided to place the case file into the quiescent category.

Five months later - months occupied with some dozens of the hundreds of cases remaining unclosed in our files - we were contemplating a vacation in the Highlands of Scotland.

It was the first Saturday in July, 1919. After partaking of Miss Hudson's weekend breakfast downstairs in her exquisite dining room - a new tradition at 221-A Baker Street- we returned upstairs to the 'B' level of 221 Baker Street.

We were enjoying a breeze through the sitting room, from the open windows and the entrance door left ajar, and the bright sunny rays angling through the bay window and exciting the dust bunnies. We were entering the frame of mind that comes upon those who have finally decided to go on a vacation.

Holmes was inspecting his fishing rods and tackle paraphernalia at his work table in the bookcase corner. "I say, Watson," he exclaimed jubilantly, "I haven't been on an extended fishing vacation since Donnithrope, in Norfolk, with the Trevors. You managed to construct the events associated with that trip into one of your recherche stories."

"I am guilty as charged, Holmes," I replied jocularly. "It was ages ago when I wrote, The Adventure of the Gloria Scott."

I put my cup of tea on its saucer and reached for the morning paper also on the tea table. A front page caption leaped into my attention.

Regimental Bugle Boy Kidnapped!

Reggie Hornblower, bugle boy in a Regiment of the King's Guards, was apparently abducted from his bedroom last night, sometime between the hours of midnight and five o'clock this morning, at 109 Ruckston Lane.

His disappearance confounds his parents and siblings, all of whom are dumbfounded. Scotland Yard has been called in to assist the local police with the investigation.

Bugler Hornblower has been on furlough from his regiment and is due to return to duty on July 12th. He served with the regiment in West Africa during its recent action in Nigeria.

Holmes had rushed across the room to read over my shoulder immediately following my reading aloud of the heading of the article.

"By Jove, Watson," he ejaculated, "call out the hounds. The hunt is on!"

"Right, Holmes, I'll get the file," I answered.

We both instantly recognized the particulars as relating to the bizarre reportings of Colonel McLaren five months earlier.

We were soon aboard the noon train out of Euston Station heading for Scotland. Two gentlemen of London headed out on a fishing vacation, dressed accordingly. Holmes wore the casual olive colored suit of a country gentleman, along with his trademark traveling cap. I was wearing a khaki colored sportsman's jacket and dark cord pants. We both had on walking boots in brown. Two fishing poles and a tackle box completed the guise. Although the several fishing lures festooning my associates ear-flapped headgear were the *piece de resistance* of our masquerade.

The plush comfort of second-class travel on an English train was a peerless boon, no pun intended. The ubiquitous tea and sandwich cart rolling down the aisle mimicked the clickey-clack of the train's undercarriage rolling along steel rails.

"I say, Holmes, is there a more harmonious sound in all of Europe than the sing-song of British rail rolling?"

"None there is, Watson, although the narrow gauge of the West Clare Railway produces a most agreeable symphony."

At the mention of the only railroad in the west of Ireland, may I remind the reader that Holmes has Irish ancestry, as first documented in my earlier narrative entitled, The Secret Adventure of Irish Gunrunning, and has been known to disappear from London from time-to-time.

We were traveling the high road to Scotland, as the train "gang" across the glorious fields of Britain, passing by the pristine villages of English history. Holmes was staring out the window in some sort of trance, presumably lost in a reverie unknown to wee mortals.

Twas late evening when the train pulled into Edinburgh. We hoisted our backpacks and walked to the nearest hostel. We presented ourselves as two members of the London police, off on a fishing vacation: inspectors Hemsol and Wonats. After a sound sleep and a frugal breakfast we set off on foot for the army post on the outskirts of the city.

As we made our way through cobblestone streets coming to life with emerging residents and shopkeepers and office clerks, the morning mist rose to slowly unveil the castle on a hill. We were walking swiftly, so I stopped Holmes by gripping his right forearm.

"I say, Holmes, have we time enough to walk along the Esplanade up on Castlehill?"

"If my analysis is correct the missing bugle boy has only eighteen hours to live, Watson," replied Holmes as he resumed his pace.

"If that is so, why are we on foot, and not on wheels?"

"I needed some more quiet time to ruminate on this case," he replied.

We passed Parliament Square and continued on through the Old Town, with its tall buildings of old stone, eventually reaching the outskirts within the hour. We found the Army post situated on a long lake, both named after the Highlanders' Regiment.

Suddenly, the fishing poles we were carrying looked apropos; although the proximity of the lake to the fort was no surprise to my fellow fisherman. We began to fish in a spot from which we had a commanding view of the fort entrance and the road leading to it.

Unable to contain my curiosity any longer, I burst out: "What is it we hope to accomplish from this vantage point, Holmes?"

"I intend for us to pass the next two hours fishing in this end of Highlanders Lake, Watson. This will allow me two hours in which to observe the comings and goings at the post. By noontime, if not sooner, the traffic in and out of the Highlanders Post will have decided our next move."

The morning brightened as the last wisps of dew and fog rose above the tree tops and a mild breeze stirred the surface of the blue lake. I was soon lost in a vision of lake trout rising amidst a swarm of hovering winged insects. Holmes went through the motions but never took his eyes off the post.

After about an hour the single spoken word, "Watson", from Holmes, alerted me to look up and observe a trio of African natives leaving the post. They were wearing the summer uniform of Army auxiliaries; khaki shirt and shorts.

We reeled in our respective lines, packed up our gear and began following them on the road back to the city. After about a mile they went left and disappeared into the patch of woods. We found the footpath and proceeded along it for another half-mile to a secluded glade beside a brook. A cluster of huts surprised us. We concealed ourselves in order to reconnoiter unseen.

The three uniformed natives we had followed were joined by several other natives wearing only loincloths. They all sat around a wee fire before a central hut in the cluster of five surrounding huts. They were having an animated powwow, complete with facial gestures and arm motions.

We pulled back some thirty meters without losing our surveillance capability, in order to talk unheard.

"Watson, give me your pistol!" said Holmes. "I shall maintain this watch while your return to the post. You must convince the Officer of the Day to send a squad or two of soldiers, a minimum of twelve, on the double. Tell them the missing bugle boy is alive and being held captive in the vicinity."

I made my way back to the post. At the entrance gate, I was detained in the guard hut while the private telephoned the Sergeant of the guard. The sergeant came out to escort me to the office of the Officer on Duty, one Lieutenant Hannoway. Being a Sunday, the O.D. (as the position is known in military parlance) was the ranking officer on the post. His natural caution was assuaged by my credentials, including my war wound pension card and medical doctor's identification. The lieutenant had read some of my stories in The Strand, to boot.

With my sketch of the location in his breast pocket, Lt. Hannoway called out the guard and led eleven of his men out the gate at the double. Four men were left on guard duty, including the sergeant. The Lieutenant had the glade silently surrounded by the time I got back to rejoin Holmes.

Holmes and I closed to within thirty meters of the center hut unseen. Lt. Hannoway and his men were to take the five huts set in a semi-circle, two enlisted men to rush each hut, with the Lieutenant and his eleventh soldier in reserve; at the sound of a pistol discharge by Holmes.

The signal shot triggered the charge! As Holmes and I lumbered toward the central hut, we saw the highlanders reach the five outside huts first. The three natives in uniform jumped up from beside the fire and ran in different directions: two in opposite directions parallel to the brook, one on a dead run toward the center hut.

Holmes, running ahead of me, stopped to assume the kneeling firing position and fired one well aimed shot, hitting the one native high in the back and dropping him dead at the entrance to the center hut.

Still running full speed, I stumbled into the hut taking down the entrance flap and rolling in, using my body as a battering ram for my partner just behind me. Two natives in loin cloths jumped up to repulse the intrusion but were shot dead by my trailing gunner.

A young white man was lying hog-tied on the ground behind the fallen natives who had been guarding him. He cried when he was freed. He was the missing bugle boy.

Holmes was near tears himself as we quickly extracted the kidnap victim from the scene of the carnage. Lt. Hannoway and his men had apprehended the other ten natives involved in the heinous plot. We made our way back to the post in the wake of, but under the protection of, the magnificent men of the Highland Light Infantry Regiment.

Holmes and I were able to catch the late afternoon train back to London. Military justice took jurisdiction in this bizarre situation. It was decided that the official report would make no mention of either Holmes or myself, in order to confine the case to the military justice system.

The report claimed that Lt. Hannoway and his men acted alone in the raid on the native camp; with three natives slain in the melee, and ten taken prisoner. The ten Tiv tribe members were to be returned to Nigeria to face uncertain justice. The bugle boy was reassigned to a regiment serving in the British West Indies.

The three slain natives were immediately interred, without autopsies (which would have identified revolver bullets) in the nearest paupers' field.

British military policy vis-a-vis employing native Africans in any category was revamped accordingly. The liberal policy of temporary immigration of such camp followers was quashed.

The next morning, the Monday, found us enjoying a late breakfast back home in Baker Street.

"Bloody frightful episode," I mumbled with a mouthful of my favorite scone. There was a question repeating in my mind since yesterday, yearning for expression.

"Aye, Watson. It was," replied Holmes dejectedly.

"Pardon my asking, Holmes," I began in a hesitance uncharacteristic in our companionship.

"Permit me to respond to your disquietude," he replied. "I have been remiss in fulfilling the obligations honored in the best of partnerships.

"The question vexing your mind indubitably refers to the shooting of the first native; does it not?"

"Exactly, Holmes," I answered in rising animation. "How could you have been positive enough to shoot the fleeing native? What if he had not been complicit in the cabal?"

"I could not gamble with the life of a British soldier, Watson. I knew from my research on the Tiv tribe that if the bugle boy was in that hut, the fleeing native would slay him the instant he reached him! I had to depend on probability statistics and a quick prayer to the Almighty.

"Had we not gone to Edinburgh yesterday, the bugle boy would have been the main course for breakfast in the native camp this morning!"

Editor's Note:

In the TIV tribe's creed of "akombo", the scapegoated victim is consumed in a ritual of cannibalism.

End Note.

The Secret Adventure of the Christmas Truce

The first peacetime Christmas, after four during wartime, came in December of 1918, only forty-five days after the end of WWI. During the euphoria that enveloped London, when every church bell in the country began ringing at the eleventh hour of the eleventh day in November; the brothers Holmes, Mycroft and Sherlock, agreed to meet at the Diogenes Club on Christmas Eve in the spirit of brotherly love.

Despite the unbearable anguish of the recent four year long conflict, London was in a blessed consciousness. The bells of the Armistice were ringing with a vengeance. The streets and avenues were charged with platoons of the faithful intent upon assaulting the altars of their respective churches in order to reclaim the high ground of Christian morality. Christmas, the penultimate celebration of Western Civilization, was being reclaimed from the forces of evil.

I arrived at 221 Baker Street, by cab, at half-three, after spending the day with family. I let myself in and proceeded up the flight of stairs, unnoticed by the usually vigilant Miss Hudson who was singing a Christmas carol in the dining room, behind the pocket doors normally open to the entrance hall.

"Happy Christmas, Holmes!" I greeted my longtime friend.

"Hear! Hear! Watson," he replied from his chair near the fire. "Let us drink a toast to peace. For 'another such victory and we are utterly undone'."

I had learned, over my long association with the world's greatest consulting detective, to commit to memory an eclectic assortment of proverbs, maxims, epigrams, and witticisms; thus having an arsenal from which to select ripostes to his intellectual revelations.

"'Against stupidity the gods are helpless,'" I responded, quoting Von Schiller. Holmes had quoted Pyrrhus.

"Excellent, Watson!" he exclaimed. "Brevity is the soul of wit."

I took my seat near the fire while Holmes poured us each a small snifter of Hennessy's cognac from the brandy decanter on the small table between us.

Then, raising his tumbler and himself, he spoke a toast. "I give you the King!" he ejaculated.

I stood to attention and drank the toast, before coming up with one from Dickens. "'It was always said of him, that he knew how to keep Christmas well'."

"Indeed, my friend," replied Holmes, "good people throughout the British Empire are quoting Dickens this Christmas Eve."

We passed the brandy and the time till high tea in a reverie known only in the myths and legends of these British Isles.

Miss Hudson served us high tea in her dining room, but only after intercepting us, each in turn, under the sprig of mistletoe which she had hung under the archway over the sliding pocket doors.

By five o'clock we had destroyed the high tea, retreating upstairs with the few leftovers. At five-ten we were in a hansom cab headed for Regent Circus and our half-five appointment with Mycroft Holmes at his club. The Diogenes Club is just opposite Mycroft's lodgings in Pall Mall (as I described in more detail in The Adventure of the Greek Interpreter).

A doorman bedecked in brass and blue escorted us up into the members' lounge on the second floor. Mycroft had effectively cordoned off a corner of the room inside a bay window, by a judicious placement of three mahogany leather chairs. Several dozen chairs of the same manufacture were located rather haphazardly about the wood-paneled chamber. A half-dozen were occupied by upper-class men enjoying solitary pursuits.

Mycroft greeted us in the hushed tone expected of club members. "Happy Christmas, Sherlock! Happy Christmas, John!"

"Likewise, older brother," replied Holmes.

"And a happy Christmas to you!" said I.

Responding to an unseen hand signal, a waiter appeared. "Bring us each one of our finest brandies," said Mycroft to the waiter.

Then, with a wave of the arm, Mycroft directed our focus to the majestic hall festooned for the Christmas holiday. All the trappings of a century of world domination were present in the room, including; regimental flags, naval banners, multicolored murals and mosaics, silver garlands and golden-framed portraits, plush carpet and eastern rugs, and one colossal crystal chandelier in the center of the oblong hall, family crests adorning the wood panels on the walls of plaster, wainscoting around the ceiling, tiny Christmas pine trees set on each tea table, and pine boughs and holly scattered around the magnificent chamber. The club leitmotif prohibiting women called for the absence of mistletoe.

When the brandies came, we began a series of toasts, starting with the King, and on down to Christmas and the concept of world brotherhood. Reflections in the brandy snifters, from and to the eyes of the brothers, Holmes, foretold of a psychic link into another dimension. No place for mere mortals.

Church bells began ringing at six in overlapping octaves of joy. Their pealing resonated in the deep segment of my memory where Charles Dickens resides. His celebrated Christmas Carol flashed into my recall memory.

"I give you Charles Dickens!" I offered a toast. We three sipped our brandies and I continued to speak. "He will live forever in the Christmas tradition of the English-speaking world!"

Mycroft's face flashed the emotional state triggered by the light of insight. "Amen. Shall we begin our own holiday custom of experiencing an evening of chronicles in Dickensian themes?" he said.

"A brilliant sentiment, brother Mycroft. Will you be our first raconteur?" asked Sherlock.

"I believe I shall, brother Sherlock. Do you remember the summer holiday we spent in Ireland when we were lads? You were only seven and I was fourteen. We rode the coach from Dublin to Killarney in the west of Ireland, in County Kerry. All during the journey you chatted on about the leprechauns of Ireland and how you were determined to see them.

"The year was 1861 and the War Between the States had only begun in America. Only a dozen years had passed since the Great Famine had decimated Ireland.

"We stayed with a local family named O'Keeffe. The Missus of the house was known to be a pleasant woman with children of her own gone to America. All but one; her son Sean, was about your age. You and Sean became inseparable chums. You enlisted him in your crusade to find 'the little people' and the pair of ye roamed all the fields and glens within a half-day's walk of the village.

"Myself, I spent quiet days reading and studying advanced courses in mathematics and the sciences. In the late afternoons after tea time, I would walk out to the local Castle and back, by the big lake. Occasionally a jaunting car would trot past, transporting an English traveler out to the lake from the inn in Killarney. A trickle of English travelers came and went with the seasons, mainly to see the lakes of Killarney, the Ring of Kerry and the Gap of Dunloe. The odd visitor came to see the abandoned famine villages.

"You and Sean O'Keeffe eventually found the great manor on the lake in Aghadoe townland, about three miles outside the village. Each day for a week, you two scampered out to Aghadoe. Whispers and sideway glances became your companions each evening in the O'Keeffe cottage. The mystery was solved when Mrs. O'Keeffe found a dwarf asleep on the turf piled against the cottage, early one morning. She brought him in to surprise you two rapscallions at breakfast. He was sitting by the fireside when you and Sean came down from the sleeping loft that morning.

"Mrs. O'Keeffe had gotten the story out of the dwarf by bribing him with tea and scones by the fire while you were still sleeping. His name was Declan and he lived in the turf shed out at the Aghadoe demesne. He was one of the local characters of Killarney reputed to be touched by the fairies.

"Declan the dwarf was invited to come in for supper each evening during our stay. Mrs. O'Keeffe opined that a good christian should not dine alone on a turf pile eating table scraps smuggled out to him by two vagabond boys. He was also invited to sleep on the earthen floor by the fire each night, but he preferred to sleep outdoors.

"For the remainder of our extended holiday in Killarney, you and Sean and Declan would abscond from the reality of cottagers' life each day. Dale and dell, dingle and glen, defile and gap, gill and gully, coulee and cleft, hollow and ravine; roaming the terrain of the region of Killarney in the company of a dwarf, who was only once-removed from the little people of Ireland, seeking to find a leprechaun.

"On our last evening there, Mrs. O'Keeffe prepared a plentiful meal of potatoes served six ways to Sunday, along with the crops gleaned by you three from the grounds of Aghadoe earlier that day. For dessert we had blackcap berries and cow's milk cream; afterwards became the magical hour in the west of Ireland, when in every cabin and cottage the oral tradition of telling stories, historical tales, chronicles of culture, family clan accounts, and recounting of local humor and gossip still prevails.

"Declan the dwarf agreed to narrate his favorite *megillah*, but only after much arm-twisting. It was a Christmas story. He promised us his tale was true."

"'Twas the night before Christmas, it was'" the dwarf began as he stared into the turf fire. 'Oi had slept all afternoon in de cellar of de big house out on de grounds of Aghadoe, next to de furnace. Himself, Lord Aghadoe, demands Oi spend de winters in de cellar. Okay, so, Oi took up de buffalo hide Oi was sleeping on...twas loaned to myself each winter by herself, Lady Aghadoe, for to keep meself warum...and Oi wore it like a cloak over me shoulders. Oi walked to the fartherest corner of de estate, to where the woodsman's cottage was, in a wee dell before de big woods. Oi was on me way to peep into de cottage to see the woodsman's family have hot chocolate and cookies by de fireplace. Afterward dey would be sure to sing Christmas carols.

"'As Oi was coming through a patch of pines, a glow from a clearing befront de cottage arose before me own oiuys. Oi dropped down and covered meself with de buffalo hide. As oi crawled de last couple yards to de edge of de clearing, Oi began hearing music and singing. Den Oi noticed dat de dell was alive with de little people.

"'A jamboree of fairies was taking place before me own oiuys! Pixies and nixies were dancing with elves in center field under a huge ball of soft light dat lit up de whole clearing butcept de cottage. Tiny sprites only six inches tall were frolicking just a couple yards befront meself, leppin about in grass nearly their own height. Leprechauns in their traditional garb were playing fiddles and flutes becenter de group of fairies. Brownies were befriending all present. Gnomes were sitting on wee logs smoking long pipes and foot-tapping in time to de music. Imps and gremlins were singing in a soft harmony from de part of de field befar de cottage. All de good people of Oirish legend were present, including de little people, de wee folk, de fairy folk and de elfin folk.

"'Oi was stretched out on de grass with me chin resting nicely on me crossed arms and me head peepin out from under de buffalo robe. Oi was verry comfortable. After a while the air was filled with the sparkle of fairy dust, like moonbeams, and all de little people began to slow down in their dancin, leppin and frolickin. Then I fell to sleepin.

"'When Oi woke it was morning light and they was all gone. There was a doubt in me mind whether the fairy visit was real or not. Perhaps it was only a dream. So, that is me story and this is the first tellin of it.'"

Mycroft sat back in his armchair and became his taciturn self. We both looked to Sherlock for a response. It soon came.

"Marvelous story, brother," said Sherlock. "I haven't recalled it for many years. Now I shall also hark back, but to a more recent Christmas experience, which also has never been told."

We all three sipped our brandy in unison and then settled back into the red leather armchairs.

"The King summoned me," Sherlock began. "The year was 1914, the first of the tumultuous war years. I was escorted by the palace guard from the front gate into the inner recesses of Buckingham Castle. He received me in his private office for a private consultation.

"The war that was to be won by Christmas was bogged down in the trenches with no end in sight. The casualties were mounting steadily. The King requested that I travel to the front to assess the situation for him. He was particularly concerned with the morale of the men.

"The next morning found me on a navy patrol boat speeding over the channel to le Havre. A royal pass signed by the King of England safely tucked inside my breast pocket. A temporary commission in the Royal Navy as a captain in the medical corps, with the appropriate uniform, was granted to my person. In the event of my capture by the enemy, however unlikely, I would not be executed as a spy who was operating behind the lines while dressed in civilian clothing. I was heading for the front.

"Once landed in France, I commandeered a staff car and driver and ordered him to drive me to Paris. En route I enjoyed an excellent lunch derived from the foodstuffs packed in my medical bag. The gods were kind, and the roads passable, and I was able to visit the Louvre during the hour before closing. My grandmother, Vernet, sister of the famous artist, was my inspiration. I had supper and spent the night in an unassuming pension on the Left Bank, opposite Notre Dame.

"In the morning, after a continental breakfast of coffee and croissants, I crossed over the Seine and walked to military headquarters in the *Place de la Concord*. A passerby had given me the location."

Holmes had perceived a look of quizzical confusion on the face of Mycroft that began when the story landed in France. Holmes realized that Mycroft remembered that the British Expeditionary Force was fighting in Belgium during December of 1914.

"Forgive this interruption to the flow of my narrative, my friends," said Holmes, with a touch of chagrin rarely displayed, "but I must explain an apparent untrueness, without revealing the entire truth behind it.

"The King had sent me on a double mission. First and foremost, I was to hand-carry a personal, sealed letter from the King to the commander of the French Forces, General Joseph Joffre, in Paris. Fortunately, the general was away from his headquarters. In the event of his absence, I was authorized to give the letter to the ranking officer at the French military headquarters in Paris. Had Joffre been present and written a reply letter, I was to carry it back to London immediately.

"My secondary mission was to visit with the BEF and to assess their morale. They were fighting outside Ypres in Belgium, a hundred miles from Paris on the crow's wing. From the main train station in Paris, I left that afternoon for Calais, a port on the English Channel about fifty miles west of Ypres.

"Next morning I was on a supply truck en route to the front, just east of Ypres. The BEF was being supplied from England, via across the channel to Calais and then by truck to Ypres.

"The front at Ypres consisted of a system of trenches in a semi-circle to the east of town. The Belgian Army occupied the northern quadrant; the BEF and a few French divisions held the southern quadrant.

"I was gallantly received at BEF headquarters by the Commander-in-Chief, Sir John French. His own morale, my first study, had been enervated and debased by the appalling casualties inflicted upon his soldiers since the war began, only four months ago. I would later recommend that he be relieved of his command.

"In retrospect, I should confess to pondering a prejudice against Sir John French; a prejudice engendered by the fate of the British 7th division, England's very best. After only one month in theater, including three weeks of continuous battle at Ypres, it's 12,000 men and 400 officers had been reduced to fewer than 2,500 men and 50 officers.

"I had arrived on the 23rd of December. Intermittent shelling was occurring at the front, a few miles to the west, coming from the German rear inside Belgium and flying on parabolic trajectory into the Allied front inside France. All told, German attacks had slackened since November.

"I was billeted in a mansion on the western edge of town with the English officers wounded in action and the medical corpsman and nurses of the BEF. The shelling continued throughout the night in a staccato reminiscent at times of the *War of 1812 Overture*.

"Christmas Eve morning I had breakfast with the medical staff. The casualties had been diminishing in the week leading up to Christmas thereby negating the need to call upon the services of a counterfeit captain in the medical corps.

"Mid-morning found me riding out to the front in the front passenger seat of an ambulance. We stopped beside a ditch that sloped down into a trench. The driver and another medic extracted two stretchers from the back of the vehicle and entered the trench leading to the front line trench system, with myself in their wake. We were walking in an auxiliary excavation used to funnel troops in and out of the front line trenches without their being exposed to small arms fire. This sunken passageway was about eight foot wide and six foot deep. Our progress was hampered by the frozen mud puddles and deep molded boot prints covering the rough earthen floor. During the quarter-mile trek an occasional enemy shell landed nearby while the echo of rifle fire sandwiched between machine gun outbursts sounded ahead.

"The landscape at the front line trenches of the BEF encompassed a view of the enemy trench system about a quarter mile westward in a matching semi-circle. In between the opposing forces rests a repose of death. Corpses lie akimbo in shell craters that blot out the character of the land; a surrealistic impression of the handiwork of the devil.

"My two stretcher-bearer companions began hauling out the current crop of casualties. I began making my way along the labyrinthian gorge eight feet below the surface of No-Man's-Land. Some English soldiers were in elevated firing positions dug into the earthen walls; mainly observers and snipers. The wounded were made comfortable along the base of the trench walls. The dead lay where they died. Small, man-sized cavities had been dug in the earthen walls, near the trench floor, into which a soldier was able to abscond when the whine of an incoming shell was heard. The bulk of England's and Ireland's and Scotland's and Wales' fighting men were living in these rat holes.

"I fell in with a company of Irish troops and spent the afternoon among them. They were all from County Clare, in the west of Ireland. They spoke of home, and of Christmas Eve, and of family, and of a short war. The shelling and sniper fire from the Germans continued to diminish as the afternoon went on.

"At precisely six o'clock as twilight fell, a bell sounded from down inside a cavity in the Irish section of the trench. Then a murmur of men with Irish accents began to be heard. The Irish Catholics were praying the Angelus. Soon the praying spread down the trench system. The English speaking soldiers of the British Empire were praying to Almighty God. More bell-like sounds resounded up and down the ungodly trenches until the harmonics of intercession began rolling across No-Man's-Land.

"At the cessation of the Angelus, a booming silence covered the battlefield. The shelling had ceased and the rifles were silent. For the next fifteen minutes soundlessness prevailed. Our men had come up out of their redoubts and began peering over the ramparts. All the guns were silent.

"The magnificent silence was barely interrupted by the strain of a melody coming from the German trenches. A German baritone was singing a familiar tune, but singing in German. His comrades began to join him. They were singing their version of *Silent Night*. The Christian Huns were soon singing all along the front. The magic of Christmas had descended upon the domain.

"Tomas O'Gorman, redoubtable sergeant, was the first man out of the English trenches. I was the second. He led the way in the dark as we scouted out the killing ground. We carried a flag of truce, a clean white undershirt of mine, hoisted atop a swagger stick. Halfway across we met several German soldiers carrying a white towel on a shovel handle. Soon we were laughing and calling out to our comrades to join us. Slowly the trenches on both sides began coughing up their battle-weary men, *sans* their weapons.

"The fraternization took on many dimensions. English soldiers brought out wine and bread; German soldiers brought out schnaps and brote. A German began playing an accordion while seated on a cadaver. An immense joy was being experienced without it's usual concomitant vocalization. But the exhausted denizens of the long graves-in-waiting, visited one another's trenches and sang Christmas carols together. Some fell asleep in the enemy trench.

"The moral tradition of Christendom had risen from the hearts and minds of it's prodigal sons and taken the field without firing a single shot. The Christmas Truce of 1914 brought peace to the battle of Ypres during WWI."

Afterwards, when Mycroft had been deposited home, Holmes and I were driven back to Baker Street in a four-wheeler during a snowfall that had begun while we were inside the Diogenes Club. Upon arrival we each gave the coachman a pound note as a Christmas consideration and scampered inside after a dash through the falling snow.

Miss Hudson had a fire going in our sitting room. We hung up our coats and warmed by the flaming turf. With the drapes drawn and a single gas lamp lit, I gazed into the fireplace and thought of Holmes' story and of the dark cavities down in the trenches he had visited.

"One thing puzzles me, Holmes," I said in a voice enveloped in awe. "How did even a single British soldier in those unspeakable trenches happen to have a bell in his possession? The single bell that rang to start the Irish troops to sing the Angelus."

Before he could answer, Miss Hudson came in with a pot of tea and poured us our cups. Then she scurried back downstairs to continue decorating the Christmas tree in her parlor.

With a sparkle in his eyes rarely ignited, Holmes revealed the answer to my conundrum. "It was Miss Hudson's dinner bell!" he said with immense pleasure.

Editor's Note:

No rain fell on Christmas Day, 1914, at the British sector of the Western Front; nor did any ammunition. In some places the truce lasted several days.

End Note.

The Secret Adventure of the Banaly Woman

"The speed of perception, also called 'acumen', has no direct relationship to the magnitude of the intuition, Watson."

Having spoken, Holmes resumed the meditative state he had been experiencing prior to making his pronouncement. Unlike ordinary voicers of opinion and impression, the sage of Baker Street issued edicts and dictums.

I poured myself another cup of tea and put aside the book I had been reading. I made a mental note regarding this new percipience to come from my associate; the latest in a series that began with the introduction of green tea into our routine by Mrs. Hudson. For, although a wit once remarked that 'black tea drinking' was the secret weapon by which the British ruled the world during the nineteenth century, the 'green tea drinking' Chinese have amazed the western world since the journeys of Marco Polo.

The first pot of tea served each day by Mrs. Hudson was now a pot of green tea, ever since the advent of spring three months ago. Today was the first day of summer, 1899. The avowing, uttering and vocalizing by Holmes, erupting from his unconscious mind while in a meditative state, during three months, or one season, of green tea drinking had motivated me to begin compiling his *bon mots* into a compendium, to be called The Laws of Sherlock Holmes.

"The science of sleuthing must incorporate the apparent art form that we have come to known as serendipity, a misnomer coined in ignorance." So spoken, Holmes came full awake, stretching his arms upward and sounding the morning moan of the well slept.

"Welcome back, Holmes," I answered facetiously. "I trust your journey to the land of Nod was pleasant."

"If only mankind would meditate, Watson, it would elevate the species."

The 'green tea oracle' then ceased to spout, receding back to whence it came. Dare I try to concatenate the sleeping prophet subconscious with the conscious mentality of the wizard of Baker Street?

"What role does the common hunch play in the theater of your science of reasoning?" I asked.

Holmes sat back in his armchair and fixed a steady gaze upon me. "Perspicacity is a trait of yours that I have come to depend on, my friend. I pray this anomalous question will be the orphan of exception in the discourse of our amity."

This bonhomous admonishing was spoken affably, so as no to prickle my feelings. Nonetheless, I became mute with chagrin.

"My dear Watson," said Holmes, "you must excuse this instance of guarded thinking on my part. Your question is legitimate and calls out for an answer.

"There is some unexplainable relation between a hunch on the one hand and a deduction or inference on the other. The former to the latter as art is to science. I have observed this phenomenon in my work, but I can not explain it."

We passed the remainder of the morning enjoying solitary enterprises. Holmes doing research in his files and notes; myself listening to a robin's outcry and daydreaming about the pleasures of summertime in the English countryside.

Mrs. Hudson had a passion for the four seasons of each year. The first day of each quarter was celebrated in epicurean delight downstairs in her dining room, which was thrown open to an eclectic fraternity of those in the working class who did her bidding. The public festivities began at one o'clock and continued unabashed until three. A private lunch for Holmes and myself, served upstairs, always began at noon and ended at twelve forty-five with Holmes and I absconding the premises via the rear garden in order to avoid the vagabondage of 'Jimmy-come-earlys' mobilizing in the front of the building.

The grandfather clock downstairs began sounding the twelve bongs of noontime. Before the last toll, Mrs. Hudson had the wine and cheese tiffin set up before us on the rolling salver cart.

"Gentlemen," she began, "the wine of the summer in this year of our Lord, 1899, is from the Banaly vineyard in the South of France."

We bolted down the rear lane at twelve forty-six and began a jaunt to the London Library at St. James' Square. The evening fog had been dissipated in the summer sunlight which had produced a surface temperature nearing eighty degrees Fahrenheit. Halfway, we paused to drink water at a baroque public drinking fountain in Grosvenor Square. The heat of the day slowed all traffic, foot and horse. When we arrived at the library, I went in to rest and read; Holmes went on to pay an impromptu visit to his brother at Mycroft's Pall Mall lodgings, across St. James' Square. Later on, Holmes met me out front of the library at half-three and we took a cab back to Baker Street for high tea at four o'clock.

The brick and stone residences along Baker Street had been designed to retain heat in winter and to repel heat in summer. Our reentry into 221 Baker Street via the rear lane and garden was undertaken as a precaution against encountering any rogues and rapscallions in post-party shivaree.

The cooler interior welcomed us in refreshing silence as we pussyfooted in; two sojourners returning to Elysium. Once upstairs, we slumped into our respective armchairs to await a teatime resuscitation.

Among the punctilios governing Mrs. Hudson's character, teatime discipline was dominant. Four o'clock tea was an English consuetude, long withstanding. It required the arrival of the Prince of Wales to disrupt the punctuality of tea time at 221 Baker Street. A momentous event that I hope to chronicle one day, should I obtain Holmes' accedence.

Mrs. Hudson wheeled the serving cart in and mentioned the letter in the salver tray. Holmes scoffed up two sandwiches before opening the letter. It read as follows:

---

17 June 1899
South Of France

Professor Sherlock Holmes:

Would you be interested in preventing a murder? If so, kindly meet me in the reading room of the British Museum this Friday, 23rd of June, at noon. I will recognize you.

A damsel in distress

"What do you envisage, Watson? The postmark is from Lyon. What can we excogitate to fill in the blanks of this mysterious request?"

"A contrivance on the part of the letter writer is apparent; perhaps some deviant motive, also," I replied.

"Is there a soul in the entire British Isles who would address me as 'professor'?" answered Holmes. "Your tales of my *nulli secundis* exploits have been responsible for a veneer of celebrity in the mind of the public, which has elevated the name, 'Sherlock Holmes', into the pantheon of the British Empire.

"However, the ersatz godly impression of myself, when seen from the continent across the English Channel on a foggy day, can easily have been abated to the caste of 'professor'.

Additionally, the return address specifies the 'South of France' and the signature line delineates 'a damsel in distress'.

"What we have here, Watson, is a *gestalten*!"

"What in the King's name is that, Holmes?"

"Loosely translated, *gestalten* is a word in the German language meaning, 'the whole is greater than the sum of its parts'."

"Would it be the equivalent of our expression in English, 'There is more to this picture than meets the eye'?" I replied somewhat pedantically.

"Forsooth, Watson!" replied Holmes. "Your analogy is praiseworthy."

It warmed the cockles of my heart to hear my mentor commend my contribution.

Friday found us heading for the British Museum in a Hansom cab. Holmes had insisted I be his accompanier. The ever-during nemesis in the limbo of his psyche, the man called Moriarity, had returned from the island of banishment in the depths of Holmes' mind, sometime during the night of the 21st. As of this morning, the 23rd, he was nearly convinced there was danger waiting in the person of, or doing the bidding of, 'Professor' Moriarity!

"Have you remembered your pistol?" Holmes asked. He was staring out with a vacant expression while he gripped the shilleleigh laying across his lap. The cab had turned into Tottenham Court Road.

"I have it in my pocket," I replied.

"Good man, Watson."

The coachman soon halted the horse-drawn, two wheeler alongside the main entrance to the massive, Greek-columned facade of the combination library and museum. As instructed, I climbed down and proceeded inside to the great, circular reading room in the magnificent, domed hall located in the inner quadrangle. While Holmes had the cab deposit him at the side entrance to the library, I was to reconnoiter the premises leading up to, and inside of, the Brobdingnagian reading room.

The walls of the round chamber were lined with books, to a height of three stories, or thirty feet. Each upper storey was accessed via a catwalk running the inside circumference. One circuit of the lower bridge enabled me to observe all below. Professor Moriarity was not present. But one figure did stand out.

An august, buxom woman in country dress, carrying a parasol of pastel colors, was gracing the central section below with her ubiquity.

Informed of the grand lady's presence *sans* Professor Moriarity, Holmes came on the great reading room with myself in his wake. She noticed him coming in and went up to him.

"Professor Sherlock Holmes, I presume," said she, as she offered her white–gloved hand.

"Your soft French accent tells me you are from the South of France," replied Holmes, as he brushed his lips to her knuckles, "and the worried expression, despite the striking smile, informs me you are my 'damsel in distress'."

"While your countenance and demeanor would enable me to recognize you had I not seen your photo," said she.

After a short interval of mutual gazing they went off, out of earshot, to speak in private, down one of the reading rows emanating from the central information desk like spokes on a wheel.

Holmes had left me hanging in the wind, a *faux pas extraordinaire*, while he was chatting up the grand dame, apparently. Their conversing in animated gestures bespoke of being smitten (I had an unobstructed view of their *tete-a-tete*). After fifteen minutes of intimate talk they left together, she holding his arm.

Once outside, Holmes helped her into a waiting cab and waved goodbye as she was trotted away. He was holding the envelope she gave him as she was leaving; just before she delicately bussed him on his cheek.

Holmes was standing starry-eyed when I reached him.

"I say, Holmes! What a smashing lady."

"Smashing indeed, Watson," he replied. "Smashing indeed." He then whistled up another Hansom cab and we left the British Museum and returned to Baker Street. During the ride he dismissed my questioning with the familiar wave of his hand.

Once we were back home in the flat, ensconced with the accouterments of our partnership, enjoying hot cups of tea, Holmes handed me the new letter from the mysterious lady after reading it himself. It read:

---

23 June, 1899
British Museum

Professor Sherlock Holmes:

Je m'appelle Cemaill de l'ann Banaly. I live with my parents and three siblings at our family vineyard near Lyon. The Banaly estate has been in our family for three hundred years, passed down successive generations via primogeniture. My father is the first Banaly heir without a son to inherit the estate.

A family crises is at hand due to my father having been recently diagnosed with a medical condition which will render him incapable of managing his affairs.

At a subsequent family council, my father announced his decision to designate me, his oldest child, as sole heir to the Banaly estate. Soon he will be compelled to grant me power-of-attorney, while he is still able.

My step-mother, his second wife, and my three half-sisters, products of their union, have been in a state of umbrage since the patriarch's proclamation. They are capable of taking formidable action against me, I'm afraid. I base this opinion on twenty long years of living under the same roof with them.

If I should die or become permanently incapacitated, the estate would then pass on to my step-mother and her offspring. This provision, if included in the upcoming will by my father, could become the catalyst for a chain of events leading to my demise.

Your reputation as a gentlemen has enabled me to overcome my innate reluctance to reveal a personal dilemma to a virtual stranger. May I rely upon your discretion in this matter, whether or not you choose to help me?

May I become,
Your devoted protegee,
Cemaill

"By Jove, Holmes!" I ejaculated. "Mrs. Hudson's bottle of wine on Tuesday was from the Banaly vineyard in the South of France. What an extraordinary coincidence!"

"Excellent recollection, Watson," said Holmes. "When one thinks of the mathematics involved, it becomes truly mind-boggling."

"What do you mean?"

"The combinations and permutations and the calculations required to express this Banaly coincidence in mathematical format."

"Can you give me an example, Holmes?"

"Very well, Watson. Recall that we began drinking the Banaly wine on Tuesday at noon. The first letter from the Banaly woman arrived one hour later, in the one o'clock mail delivery. The probability of these two events happening to occur with near simultaneity, at a location in common, in a foreign country, approaches 'sweet Fanny Adams'.

"I'll tell you something for nothing, Watson, as the Irish are wont to say. The science of calculating and predicting outcomes is currently being developed by leading mathematicians. I am not at liberty to divulge any further statements on this new research."

I could see the handwriting on the wall (or blackboard) in this case, and it was the hand of Mycroft Holmes. Besides, I was feeling the whimwams over asking my friend about his bussing beauty of Banaly; and it was time to placate my disquietude.

"You and she shared a special moment together in the reading room, did you not?" I asked him timorously.

"'Special' is a word pregnant with synonyms, Watson. It would behoove you to be more specific when making a reference to a lady of her beseeming."

Seeing as how I was unwilling to be forced to run through the gauntlet of verbal maneuvering, which Holmes was capable of engineering as a smoke screen; I wisely elected to abort my query in order to avoid a quandary. My reply consisted of a deliberate silence.

A short pause ensued during which Holmes picked up the letter for a second reading.

"I shall be leaving for France, tomorrow," said Holmes.

"Can you arrange your affairs to allow you to be on standby, should I send for you to join me there?"

"I can and I will." I replied instantly.

When the train carrying Sir Corkshel Hemsol, wine buyer for the English royal family, arrived in Lyon Sunday morning, it was met by a four-wheeler from the Banaly Vineyards. The jarvey easily found the distinguished gentlemen detraining, who was wearing a royal blue blazer emblazoned with the crest of Windsor.

After a two-hour drive into the wine country of the Rhone Valley region, the mustachioed Sir Hemsol was deposited at the manor house of the Banaly Vineyards. The houseman was waiting to greet the guest and escort him to one of the rooms in the guest wing on the upper floor. After unpacking, Holmes (alias Sir Hemsol) was resting on the bed when the bouteillier came in to inform him of a dinner in his honor that evening.

"Welcome to the house of Banaly, Sir Hemsol," called out the pale patriarch at the far end of a long, oak dining table. Holmes had been led down to the formal dining room on the main floor by the butler (a.k.a. the bouteiller) at six o'clock.

"Greetings to the house of Banaly!" replied Holmes to all present, as he was seated between comely Cemaill and her minacious stepmother at the pallid patriarch's right hand. Across the table from them sat three cheerless teenage girls. Introductions were made and the five course meal began. The bouteillier rolled in a silver wine cart and poured from the private, family vintage of the previous harvest. The maid servant carried in a large silver tray laden with the cheeses of France. The men present proposed toasts to the Kings of England and France.

After dessert, Beatrice went to her husband's side with his medicine.

"*Excuse m'oi*, Sir Hemsol," said Banaly, "the doctor insists that I must take this awful-tasting tonic after meals."

"By all means," replied Holmes.

Beatrice deftly spooned the liquid into her husband's mouth and returned the bottle to her waistband. Then, after touching her thumb and index finger to her lips, she kissed him full on the mouth, as they do in France.

"*Pardonez m'oi*, Sir Hemsol," said Banaly, weakly. "I must now retire for the evening. My first daughter, Cemaill, will entertain you. You must be eager to visit our wine cellar."

The Banaly manor house was constructed in the mid-eighteenth century, before the French revolution of 1789. Its stone and mortar architecture was typical of the period. One end of the long rectangular structure was abutted by a nearby hillock. It was under this barrow where the wine cellar was concealed.

Cemaill led her guest out into the secluded flower garden beyond the dining hall annex. Hidden by hedgerows the garden went unperceived by the tramontane. Under a bower at the far end, Cemaill broke the silence with a sudden whirlabout and an audible sigh.

"*Sacre bleu*," she murmured, throwing her arms around her guest. *"Mon cheri*, I would recognize you in any masquerade!"

"I saw the bonfire in your eyes when I entered the dining room," Holmes replied.

"I detected your stride and your posture," she giggled.

"My sword is yours to command, m'lady," smiled Holmes, surrendering to a sudden impulse of whimsey.

With a graceful pirouette, Cemaill did a curtsy to reveal a hidden portal. She lifted open the sod-covered door and beckoned for Holmes to follow. She lit a candle and they disappeared behind the grass hatch.

As I recount this excerpt of Sherlock Holmes' second meeting with the 'Banaly Lady', the reader will realize that I can only relate what details Holmes has divulged to me. Whatever else transpired between the aspiring couple, especially down in the wine cellar, is known only to the pair of them; except for the contents of the following telegram:

South Of France
Banaly Estate
Monday, 26 June 1899

Dr. Watson

Gather all research on slow-acting poisons. Bring same with you. Depart London on Tuesday afternoon, via my itinerary on desk. Arrive next morning.

Sir Hemsol

P.S.

Wine bottle tampering has taken place.

Monday morning early, Holmes knocked up Cemaill, as per her instructions. When she was dressed, they went downstairs for a breakfast of French toast and tea, served on the outdoor patio.

The coachman had been sent off to post a telegram, so Cemaill and Holmes walked arm-in-arm the half-mile distance to the grape processing facility on the grounds.

Three huge wooden vessels, barrel-like, were being loaded with freshly picked, red grapes. The three half-sisters were standing by ready to begin stomping the grapes. Nadon, the oldest sister, followed by Sareeth and Joymar, went up steps to a platform which girded the vats. Barefooted, they each climbed into their usual tank to begin the daily smushing. Italian music began playing from a speaker mounted on the outside wall of the barn-like warehouse across the grey estrade. The upper torso of each girl was visible, rising and falling to the beat of the music. It was not until the Tarantella was played that a freshet of the juice of the grapes began to trickle down the outlet pipes into smaller brown barrels at ground level.

Holmes and the Banaly woman returned to the manor grounds, after a lovers' tour of the woodland at the eastern edge of the demesne, in time for lunch on the outdoor patio with Cemaill's father, as planned. Sir Hemsol took the occasion to announce his approval of the Banaly vineyards as the newest winery to the Royal Family of England. Lord Banaly's countenance was one of joyance and mirth modulated by paleness and tranquility.

Lady Beatrice, who had been cutting fresh flowers in her garden beyond, joined them for a dessert of tea and crumpets. When her husband was ready to leave she repeated her wifely routine performed after each meal; giving her husband his medicine and kissing him full on the mouth, before leading him off to rest either in his den or in their bedroom.

Cemaill complied with Sir Hemsol's desire to tour the flower garden. Afterwards they 'rested before dinner' (Holmes' exact words to me).

Holmes spent the following day, a Tuesday, as a jarvey; driving Miss Cemaill the breadth of the province in her pony and trap, with an intermission for a picnic lunch in a remote glade, alone with mother nature.

When I arrived in Lyon on Wednesday morning, Holmes was but a cheerful and relaxed revenant of his habitual self. The inveterate investigator of my long acquaintance was being impersonated by an insouciant imposter. He had been driven to the train station by the coachman, as Sir Hemsol, for his return to London. He booked into a nearby hostel, instead, as Sherlock Holmes; returning to meet my train's arrival.

We had lunch in the side garden of the hostel, underneath a shade tree that was growing there at the time of the French revolution.

"It's grand to see you, my good friend!" said Holmes.

"I came as quickly as possible, Holmes."

"Yes, my faithful comrade," beamed Holmes, "as I was certain you would. I see you brought me the research I requested."

I passed the dossier I was carrying across the wooden table to him. As he perused the contents, I partook of the sapid *hors d'oeuvre* served with a Chablis of the region. Holmes joined me in the repast while he continued to read. I fed some sparrows with the crumbs off the table. A plaque in sunlight on the side of the inn claimed that the local leaders in the revolution often dined here during the days of the guillotine.

"Eureka, Watson!" Holmes suddenly cried out. "You have brought me the confirmation."

"What was the issue?" I responded casually.

"The bone of contention, my ingenuous confidant, revolves around a slow poisoning; a dastardly crime which appears to be occurring at the Banaly manor.

"Prompted by the fear of disinheritance and motivated by greed, the second wife of Lord Banaly, Beatrice nee Capriccio, has cultivated a mildly toxic flower, indigenous to her native Sicily, and known as the 'breath freshener'. Traditionally masticated by lovers, the level of toxicity is easily repulsed by the natural defenses of the human body. But this immunity weakens over time allowing a slow poisoning to occur over a continuous exposure. Ingested sparingly, this 'kissing flower' is reputed to have the ability to elevate the passions; an aphrodisiac, if you will.

"Lady Beatrice practices a dosology of deceit upon her trusting husband. She concludes his every meal with the prescribed dosage of a liquid as prescribed by his doctor, and kept inside a cumberbund about her waistline. This is followed by a lover's kiss which delivers the 'breath freshener', allegedly as an antidote to the bitter taste of the legitimate medicine.

"She carries crushed petals of this kissing flower inside the same cumberbund. Each time she returns the medicine bottle therein, she takes a pinch of the mortared crush to her lips with thumb and forefinger before delivering the mortiferous osculation.

"I don't mind telling you, Watson, that the fathoming of this scheme presented me with a minimum of difficulty. However the *sina qua non* of my assistance in this familial fiasco requires a solution which will retain this family in harmony. Not one which will involved the incarceration of any family members. My client is adamant on this point."

"Has the Lady Cemaill recanted the fear of family violence against herself, should she become sole heir?" I asked.

"Now that her father's health will be restored, she is willing to let bygones be bygones, assuming I can provide a plan which will protect the family name without jeopardizing family members."

"And have you?" I asked. "Such a contrivance would outclass the concoction of the comely creatrix, the Lady Beatrice," I added lightheartedly.

"Flippancy becomes you, Watson," a grinning Holmes replied. "Some comic relief is always welcome, when it is injected apropos; *comme il faut.*

"The Lady Cemaill and I do have a conception in mind; one that will entail regular visitations by myself, in order to guarantee a successful conclusion to this tension. More than this I an unable and unwilling to divulge; neither to you nor to your readers!"

The Secret Adventure of the Piltdown Fossils

Within the canon of these ‘secret adventures’ there lies dormant an anecdote especially embarrassing; primarily to myself, only secondarily, if at all, to Sherlock Holmes. That said, it is the one story I have been eager to forget ever happened. Holmes, on the other hand, has been encouraging me to write an account of it, for therapeutic reasons, and for the historical record; the therapy to benefit myself, the history is for Holmes.

My trepidation is offset by my intrepid associate, who empowers me to begin this tale.

“Look here, Watson,” said Holmes, as he passed me the Manchester Guardian, “paleontology has a new cast member making his debut at a site in Sussex.”

According to the article, fossils of the skull of a prehistoric man-ape had been found recently near Piltdown Common, in Sussex, by one Charles Dawson.

When I looked up from the morning newspaper, Holmes had left the room. A thin stream of vapor was still rising from the spout of the teapot under the cozy, so I poured myself another cup of tea and sat back in my armchair to ponder.

Holmes came back in some time later to interrupt a reverie in which I was with Lord Kitchner in the Sudan in 1898. "Awake, Watson," he said casually, "*Carpe diem*!"

At the fireplace, he placed a peat on the fire and selected one of his cherished pipes from atop the mantlepiece before settling down in his armchair nigh mine.

"The theory of evolution gathers more credibility in some quarters with each new fossil discovery of a prehistoric creature," he continued on, somewhat sceptically, "I recall the brouhaha that resulted back in 1889 when Eugene DuBois found the fossils of 'Java Man'; which the scientific community has since renamed '*Pithecanthropus Erectus*'; meaning 'man-ape who stands erect'."

"My skepticism concerning evolution is profound, Holmes; a severity of doubt which lies outside the bounds of my experience."

"Pyrrhonism is not a deviant response," Holmes answered, "to a theory so foreign to man's intuitive intelligence."

Pretending to know the definition of the word, 'pyrrhonism', I said: "The Geological Society has its next meeting in December. Let us wait and see what the membership and the ruling committee have to say about this Piltdown fossil."

Editor's Note:

On December 18th, 1912, Charles Dawson presented his find, 'Piltdown Man', to the Geological Society of London. The group, comprised of the leading figures in geology and in paleontology, validated the discovery by assigning it the formal scientific name, *'Eoanthropus dawsoni'* (Dawson's dawnman). They declared it to be a genuine human ancestor.

End Note.

By the summer of the following year, 1913, the furor over the theory of evolution had reached all levels of British society. While the learned and priviledged mostly believed in the theory, the commoners and the cornerboys dismissed it as preposterous.

Meanwhile, the residentiary of 221-B Baker Street had been conducting a continuous commentary on the pros and cons of the revolutionary hypothesis.

"Look here, Holmes," I blurted out to my companion who was tinkering with test tubes at his laboratory table, "the logic of evolution is irrefutable, is it not? Do we not agree that the mechanism of 'natural selection', as presented by Darwin in The Origin of The Species, is well-founded?"

"The feck of the process of 'natural selection' is manifest, my easygoing friend," replied Holmes, "but the extrapolation-to-certainty cannot efface the common sense inherent in the human mind. The enigma of creation remains! Who created the process, or design of, 'natural selection'?"

One was always on boggy ground when differing with the world's greatest sleuth, so I threw in my metaphorical towel. "Let's have another cuppa tea, my even-tempered confederate."

"Spendid, Watson,", said Holmes, "The conundrum of creation can keep through teatime."

As we were savoring the last morcels of home-baked scones, the postman rang the doorbell. Mrs. Hudson came up with a letter. It follows:

---

2 June 1913
Sussex

Dr. John H. Watson
221 Baker Street
London

Permit me to introduce myself. I am a fellow medical doctor, as well as a fellow short story writer. I have a small practice a few miles from Barkham Manor, where the Piltdown Man fossil was found. A prominent scientist has commissioned me to investigate the 'Piltdown fiasco' (his very own words).

My paleontological experience and forensic training have prompted my selection to undertake this quest; although I am of the mind that you were the better choice. I have read some of your Adventures With Sherlock Holmes; your experiences therein are nonpareil.

Would you consider a collaboration with me on a post-mortem of Piltdown?

Most Sincerely,
Dr. A. C. Doyle

Holmes erupted from his chair with excitement, exclaiming, "Simultaneity again, Watson. Coincidence is becoming the byword of 221 Baker Street."

"Shall I respond to Dr. Doyle in the affirmative?" I asked.

"By all means do. I will be on standby should you request my subvention."

After sleeping on it overnight the question of how to respond to Dr. Doyle's flattering letter I sent off the following telegram in the morning:

221-B Baker Street
London
4 June 1913

Dr. A. C. Doyle
Sussex

Unless otherwise notified, will arrive Sussex morning train June 7.

Dr. John H. Watson

Holmes and I made an impromptu visit to the British Museum in the afternoon. He insisted that I bone up on the bare essentials of the fossil record, before my trip to Sussex. It was good of Holmes to be concerned; no need to embarass 'the partnership' (as he sometimes called us). He also suggested that I take along one of his choice axioms; namely, to 'say little, listen much'.

Friday morning found me at Victoria Station, on the platform, waiting to board the train to the midlands. Holmes had shared the cab with me before continuing on to Scotland Yard, via Victoria Street, where he had scheduled an early appointment with Inspector LeStrade's successor; concerning a matter that 'did not concern me', in Holmes' own words. I suspected he was feeling a bit put out as the result of being relegated to the status of 'back-bencher' for the first time in our good-fellowship. After all these years together, I was still getting to know my compatriot.

A welcoming party was waiting for my late-morning arrival at the Sussex station. Along with Dr. Doyle, I met Charles Dawson and Father Pierre Teilhard de Chardin. The introductions had no lack of genuine gusto and sincere *bon homie*. Eventually, Dr. Doyle's coachman saw to it that we were all safely seated in his four-wheeler cab and he was able to depart the station.

Within the rolling coach a conversation was taking place that had no precedent in the history of civilization on the earth. Geology, Paleontology, Religion, Philosophy, Medicine, and Logic; each represented and discussed with the spark of genius prevailing; Teilhard de Chardin's flame burning brightest, with Dr. Arthur Conan Doyle's a close second.

Charles Dawson had an intimate knowledge of the path of human evolution in as much as he had found, and synthesized into the body of human learning, the **'missing link' fossil.** The human cranium and the ape-like jaw exhumed at the Piltdown site had become singularly responsible for the shift in the public mind toward the acceptance of the theory of evolution. Although, a credentialed minority of scientists in Great Britain and elsewhere held varying degrees of skepticism, ranging from mild doubt to outright repudiation of the deviant theory.

Pierre Teilhard de Chardin, Jesuit cleric, philosopher, and collector of fossils, had only recently explored the Cro-Magnon caves of northern Spain, in June.

Remarkably, in early July, during a brief visit with Dawson here at his home in Lewes, Teilhard had the astonishing good fortune to find a **fossil tooth** at the original site in Piltdown. The long, lean, aquiline, French priest with a penetrating gaze, had managed to discover a canine tooth that fit into the ape-jaw fossil at one end and the man-cranium fossil at the other end; thereby validating the first Piltdown find (by Dawson) with the second Piltdown find (as it came to be known). Teilhard's fossil tooth became the key in the lock that opened the door of doubt, beyond which lay the proof of the process of evolution.

The scintillant conversation of the Piltdown principles was interrupted, but barely, when the cab arrived at Barkham Manor, home of the Piltdown site. We proceeded on foot to a partially dug up gravel pit out beyond the great residence, alongside a footpath. The knee-deep excavation had been staked and roped off. Dawson revealed that it took him four years to find the pieces of the human cranium that he reassembled into the skull fossil portion of his famous find; the ape-like jaw fossil, intact, had been found last. Dawson also was proud to be friends with his esteemed partner in Piltdown finds, Pierre Teilhard de Chardin; a friendship that began in 1909.

By teatime we were all safely entrenched in the living room of the country cottage of Dr. Doyle, who was finally able to get a word in edgewise as the interlocution of his intrepid guests suffered wee pauses while they drank. His countryside home was only a few miles from Barkham Manor. His lovely wife was a most gracious hostess. She managed to charm the cerebral clique with her delightful demeanor and Celtic charm.

Dawson and Teilhard left together at the half-five of twilight onboard the Doyle four-wheeler, with the coachman's assurance they would not be late for their respective destinations. And the coach clackety-clacked down the country lane, under imbricating limbs of vintage trees of the ancient forest that once overspread the dominion.

Back inside the cheerful cottage, Dr. Doyle and myself settled into snug chairs, by a wee turf fire, to ward off the chill of an evening; while the Mrs. Doyle attended to other matters, including barnyard chores and country dogs.

Doyle had had the foresight to make sketches of the pertinent fossils. He produced these vellums, along with a set of copies for me to take back to London. The actual fossils were in the custody of the British Museum. The drawings were the work of one who was mindful of the precepts of engineering drawing. We spent the early evening reviewing the drawings, which were drawn to a one-to-one scale, with some details magnified.

Later in the evening, after a nightcap of some few Irish whiskeys with Mrs. Doyle, which included the singing of some songs of Irish risings, we three retired arm-in-arm-in-arm up a bending staircase.

The following day, a Saturday, found me back in Baker Street by mid-afternoon. Holmes was out on a training exercise with the Baker Street Irregulars, according to Mrs. Hudson, but was expected home for tea at four. It gave me an extra hour to mull over my thoughts and to make up my mind about the Piltdown affair; before the inevitable third-degree I was sure to receive from my mentor.

I had unrolled the set of drawings, and weighted down the corners of the tracings, on the lab table, when a commotion out on the street brought me to the bow window. Holmes had arrived commanding a squad of his Irregulars who were marching nicely, in military order, down the center of Baker Street; about a dozen in all.

After a 'halt, one, two', followed by a 'right face', they were facing the building from curbside. Their squad leader spoke to them briefly before dismissing them and watching while they scampered in four directions. Holmes then dashed into the house and up the flight of stairs.

He burst in, feigning a military manner, and issued a direct order: "Stand to ready!" he barked, trying to conceal a smile.

"As you were, trooper!" I countered, "You forget I outrank you." reminding Holmes of my service in the Second Afghan War as a military surgeon.

"Had I not refused a Knighthood in 02, you'd not be enjoying the 'life of Reilly' in me presence, boyo." said he.

"It's a 'pawky' sense of humor ye be displaying, laddie," said meself, with a laughing lilt.

"Hoisted by my own petard," said he, referring to one of my tales, The Valley of Fear, in which he referred to my 'pawkey' sense of humor. Then he added "I must recognize a compliment when I see one," thereby getting the last word, as usual.

As if on cue, Mrs. Hudson came up with the tea. "I'll be on my way, now, for an hour or two," she remarked, "there's to be a demonstration in Hyde Park, on the question of this blasphemous theory of Mr. Darwin. All my peers will be in attendance." And off she went.

Holmes had loaded up his current favorite pipe and was pacing about with his cup of tea when he noticed the drawings.

"Yoicks, Watson, here lies the domain of the fox we must pursue. Who is the drafter of these specimens?"

"Dr. Doyle made these tracings from the original drawings done by a draftsman in the employ of Charles Dawson. The actual drawings, along with the fossils, are being kept at the museum."

As Holmes became engrossed in the drawings, I remembered his lack of standing in this case; his assistance had not been requested. It pained me to see my preceptor, the oracle of investigation, cast in disregard. On the pretence of having to run a medical errand, I went out for a walk to clear my mind.

I headed south on Orchard Street to its terminus at Grosvenor Square. To return, I walked north on Manchester Street from where it runs into the east side of Grosvenor Square. Just past the corner of Oxford Street a telegraph office gave me an inspiration. I went in and sent off a local telegram:

221-B Baker St.
8 June 1913
Saturday 5 p.m.

Mycroft Holmes
Diogenes Club
Pall Mall

Subject: Piltdown Fossils

Sherlock needs access to subject; while under the authority and auspices of some agency of His Majesty's government.

Dr. John H. Watson

Upon my return, Holmes hardly noticed; enraptured as he was with the details in the drawings. I settled in for a quiet evening of reading, to be punctuated by the occasional cup of tea. The breeze from the bow window was balmy; the sounds from the Saturday evening swells passing by were comforting.

At 8p.m. a telegram arrived.

Diogenes Club
8 June 1913
Saturday 7 p.m.

Mr. Sherlock Holmes
221-B Baker St.

Subject: Piltdown Fossils

Your analysis of subject is hereby requested.

Arthur Smith Woodward
Curator of Geology
British Museum of Natural History

Once again, Mycroft's contacts with his fellow club members provided his brother access to the highest levels of influence in both society and government.

Not surprisingly, Holmes neglected to request my accompaniment when he set out next morning; however unusual. I may have inadvertently irritated my close friend when I volunteered my opinion on the validity of the fossils in question. My line of reasoning relied upon the affirmation by the Geological Society, including their spawning of the new appellative: 'Dawson's dawn-man'. Any reasonable doubts were eliminated by the Second Piltdown Fossil, found a year later, which confirmed the basic assumption; namely that the two skull sections came from the same individual.

Editor's Note:

In the interests of unity and wholeness, the narration of this tale now switches to the inimitable Sherlock Holmes (thinking to himself)!

End Note.

After a thorough, nay painstaking, study of the tracings drawn by Dr. A. C. Doyle, I find myself in a nonplussed state of mind. My intuition, which I dislike to acknowledge, is pestering my conscious, rational mind with interruptive doubt.

The scientific community, worldwide, with few exceptions, has accepted the fossils known as Piltdown Man as genuine; and has recognized Dawson's dawn-man as a hominid ancestor of mankind on earth.

My good man, Watson, after a visit to the Piltdown site with the principles involved, has concluded that the fossils are the real McCoy. I pray he is correct in his assessment; this companion, confidant, and confederate of mine.

Editor's Note:

Watson resumes the narrative.

End Note.

Holmes spent the day at the British Museum with Woodward, examining the Piltdown fossils, before returning home for afternon tea. I came by later, about 6 p.m., to meet with the oracle of Baker Street.

When I entered the flat he had a *sui generis* look about him. In the pantheon of human expression, where a thousand faces reside, a new one was on display.

"Good evening, Holmes," said I.

"Good evening, Watson," said he.

I hung my hat on the rack behind the door and went over to my armchair, beside Holmes in his.

"I am eager to hear about Piltdown," said I.

"I am glad you are seated , my friend," he began, "for the fossils have been tampered with."

"What are you saying, Holmes?"

"I am saying that the fossils have been tampered with."

"When? How?" I asked in confusion.

"Beforehand; by a perpetrater!"

"Impossible! The British Geological Society pronounced Piltdown to be genuine."

"Notwithstanding, someone has committed an egregious fraud which has apparently hornswoggled the entire scientific establishment."

"Holmes, are you mad? Have you been smoking the opium pipe again?"

Editor's Note:

That said, Watson stormed out of the flat and they never spoke of it again; not until years had passed.

On November 19, 1953 (forty years later), two scientists: Kenneth Oakley and J.S. Weiner, using fluorine dating, determined that all three components of the Piltdown fossil: skull-piece, jaw, and interlocking canine, were only several hundred years old! Thereby proving that all three specimens had been deliberately planted at the site.

The begetter(s) of this hoax have yet to be unearthed.

End Note.

The Secret Adventure of the Irish Rising

At the risk of jeopardizing a lifelong friendship, I have decided to provide the historical record with an account of Sherlock Holmes' participation in the most significant event in the history of the little green country across the Irish Sea; namely, 'The Easter Rising of 1916'. Of the many tales in the secret adventures category, this is the one tale Holmes has banned the telling of. The sacrosanct nature of the proceedings involved has compelled me to reveal what I believe to have been my sidekick's finest hour. You, the reader, will be the final arbitrator.

Easter Sunday fell on April the twenty-third in 1916. A day of rejoicing in all of Christendom, including these British Isles. The divine nature of Jesus Christ trumping the somewhat petty differences between the various sects of Protestantism and bedrock Catholicism. The Church of England had been aborted from the Holy Roman Empire by an English king, Henry VIII, in order to slake his royal loins. Some three hundred and eighty-two years since, and despite onerous political oppression and radical penal laws, the Irish have refused to renounce their Catholicism, which dates back to Saint Patrick in the fifth century A.D.

A movement in Ireland, led by three poets, had been planned for this day. A rising of a people weary after seven hundred odd years of domination. A grab bag group of paupers, peasants, and poets were about to march on the British Empire! As Christ rose from the dead; the Irish People would rise up from subjugation.

Some rationing had been instituted as the 'war to end all wars' dragged on, but a supply of fresh eggs maintained its presence on the bill of fare at 221 Baker Street. One of the Irregulars, known by the to-name, Eggman, had a coop full of chickens behind his country cottage in an outlying district. He delivered the eggs on his bicycle several times weekly, mainly to the families of his confederates.

Good Friday of 1916 was on April twenty-first. A Ukranian repaiman arrived in mid-morning to mend the rear garden fence. He worked his way into Mrs. Hudson's kitchen by fixing the leather hinges on her window box. When we heard him banging away and her loud laughing, Holmes sent me downstairs to suss out the situation.

They were having lunch as nice as you please; egg sandwiches on toast, a garden salad, and hot tea. I declined his gracious invitation to join them and reported back upstairs.

As one of us chuckled and the other snickered, we managed to enjoy our usual lunch; afterwards supplementing our leisure with silent reading. When the clock on the mantle sounded two chimes, we suddenly realized that an odd quietude was wafting from below. I rose up in dismay and dashed downstairs. Ugo, the middle-aged , Ukranian tinker, was doing 'pysanky' with our beloved landlady. Rather than become a third eyelid in a delicate situation, I withdrew from their consociation and tread softly up the stairs.

"Holmes," I said, "you won't believe what I encountered downstairs."

"Pray tell, what would that be?"

"The Ukranian vagabond had Mrs. Hudson doing 'pysanky'!"

Holmes laughed and replied "The Ukranians are known for 'pysanky'; and tis the Easter season".

I was unable to perceive if Holmes knew what 'pysanky' meant or whether he was bluffing. "Are you not shocked to hear of our Mrs. Hudson engaging in this exotic behavior?" I asked, beguilingly.

"The hand-painting of Easter eggs can hardly be conceived of as 'exotic', Watson, regardless of one's companion in the affair."

Once again, Holmes had astonished me with the scope of his general knowledge. And once again, I had lost the word game to him.

"'Cunning' becomes you, my crafty friend," he went on, "feel free to exercise it in my direction. It can only serve to sharpen my faculties."

When the telephone rang downstairs in the entrance hall, it startled us both. Mrs. Hudson had it installed recently, at my behest, in order for me to stay in closer touch with my medical practice. Holmes maintained his preference for the written word and had yet to use the telephone downstairs, or anywhere else. She and I were hopeful that he would pay one-third of the expense, eventually; after all, Scotland Yard were using telephones now.

Mrs. Hudson took the call, from her daughter most likely. She also received calls from the local shop owners and tradespeople she dealt with. My calls were either from my goodwife or my medical practice. Holmes had yet to receive any calls – he refused to learn the telephone number – but I had acquiesced to Mrs. Hudson's request to include our new phone number in the published listing.

Shortly after the itinerant jack-of-all-trades departed the premises, a telegram arrived and Mrs. Hudson brought it upstairs to officially announce it; as was her custom.

"Telegram for Sherlock Holmes!" she said, formally, as I opened the door.

Holmes accepted the cablegram apprehensively. Two years into WWI had seen too many telegrams, sent to too many English-speaking families, bearing too many tragic 'killed in action' notices. This wire was sent from Dublin, Ireland.

It read as follows:

General Post Office
Dublin, Ireland
20 April 1916

Sherlock Holmes
London, England

Come over for an Easter visit with the rising of the moon.
Cousin Declan

"A last minute invitation, I'd say," said I.

"Exactly, Watson, which is precisely why I must be off on the evening train," said Holmes. "Be a good man and pack my bag for me while I attend to some correspondence."

"Very well, Holmes. However, the next full moon comes in a fortnight. How long will you be away?"

"I must be there for the rising of the moon!"

Holmes left in a hansom cab, shortly after tea, headed for Euston Station in an early evening fog. The North Western Railway terminus, there, anchored a railway that extended to Holyhead, in Wales, at the other end. The route was familiar to him. After crossing the English midlands the train would wind through Wales and make its way to the end of the line, near on eleven o'clock, at the ferry terminal; leaving only a short walk to a private hotel. After a sound sleep he would board the morning ferry to Dublin, enjoy some breakfast enroute, and disembark before noontime. Then but a short walk to the boarding house, where his cousin resided. I knew from experience how much fulsome pleasure he took from this journey.

My goodwife was jubilant over the prospects of having the undivided presence of her husband during the Eastertime.

We began our holiday of 'Holmes in absentia' with a quiet evening at home, in our sitting room, by the fireside; she knitting while I read a novel of the American West. Then early to bed.

Next morning, Easter Sunday, my mention of the art of hand-painting hard-boiled eggs prompted an outcry from Mrs. Watson. "Oh John, dear; you absolutely must have this Ukranian rustic in for tea."

Then, her eyes ablaze in full twinkle, she cast her *bon mot*: "Perhaps he can teach me 'pysanky', too!"

As must be obvious to you, dear reader, I had had the extreme good fortune to marry a woman who could always get a rise out of me.

Afterwards, we attended a Christian church service at noon to celebrate the rising of the Nazarian. The battle raging in France, at Verdun, was the subject of the blackcoat's sermon. The theme of which presumed that prayer to the God in Heaven, whose Son rose from the dead – the seminal event in the rise of Christendom – would effectuate victory in the war against the bloody Boche; a conflict threatening to bring down the curtain on the peace-loving peoples.

We came out of church under pealing bells into what promised to be a sunny afternoon. With a newly polished trap and a sprightly horse, we set out, side-by-side, from St. John's Wood, headed for Hyde Park, along the Edgware Road. We passed the Baker Street Station road on the left, the route so familiar to the horse, leading to Baker Street. After passing Tyburnia on the right we came to the road ending at Oxford Street. Crossing Oxford we entered Hyde Park at the site of the Tyburn Tree, famous gallows spot.

At a slow, clip-clop pace, we left the center of the wide roadway to the trotting hansom cabs and prancing four-wheelers. London society ladies were strolling along the promenade in the latest spring fashions, on the arms of men wearing bowler hats and swinging alpenstocks, in the shade of massive softwood trees.

After landing at Kingstown harbor, Oscklehr Moshel, an itinerant jew, walked through Irishtown and Ringsend Park to reach Ringsend Road, which led him to the heart of downtown Dublin. He was carrying a small portmanteau containing the belongings of Sherlock Holmes.

Moshel crossed the bridge over the River Liffey and proceeded north on Sackville Street. Passing through the most Catholic community in Western Civilization, disguised as a foreign traveller, Holmes felt remarkably at home in Dublin city. The shops and business premises along this main thoroughfare were being challenged by Dubliners scurrying about for wares and vendibles for tomorrow's Easter dinner. Shopkeepers kept a special eye on the 'shawlies', who were not above a friendly pilfer.

Continuing northwards on Dorsett Street he sought to find a boarding house within the warren of irregular lanes and rows nestled within the triangle formed by Sackville Street, Dorsett Street, and the Circular Road. The neighborhood was comprised of small, tiny, two-storey, brick row houses, each barely ten feet wide. Separated by cobblestone lanes and narrow sidewalks, the triangle district dwellings brought to mind the 'Little People' of Celtic lore and legend. Each time Holmes came across the Irish Sea to Ireland, thoughts of Erin would bubble up into his consciousness, of their own volition; unprecedented events in the mental life of the finest detective in Christendom.

After inquiring at a grocer's shop on the perimeter of the quarter, he located the address of the boarding house recommended by the merchant: 323 Backhouse Lane. The landlady, a Mrs. Picker, had been born midway through the reign of Good Queen Victoria, c. 1850. She had one other border in residence, a Mr. Cetnich, a Czech laundryman. Oscklehr Moshel paid a week in advance for the bedsitter room on the second floor front, with a window on the lane. Breakfast of tea and scone, and evening supper, was included.

Mrs. Hudson had just returned from an Easter visit with her good friend, Honora Winslow, who owned a townhome on

Manchester Street, a few blocks over from Baker. Mrs. Hudson made it her habit to be home and off the streets before dark. She was enjoying a spot of tea by the fire, in her parlour, when the telephone began to ring out in the lobby. She went out in the foyer to answer it.

"Halloo, halloo, …Yes. Hello, Mr. Holmes … Likewise …Dr. Watson is with his wife, at home, I presume … You are calling from Dublin, how nice … UH huh …uh huh … uh huh…Yes, I understand … O.K. … Yes, uh huh …O.K., I'll repeat it. You want Dr. Watson to return to Baker Street first thing tomorrow morning, and to remain here until you call again … Very well, Mr. Holmes … Uh huh … Goodbye."

Holmes let himself out of the public telephone booth, the first of its kind to be installed in Dublin, outside the General Post Office, on the west side of Sackville Street. It was twilight and the telephone enclosure was flush with the building's façade, tucked behind one of the massive Greek columns supporting the tetrastyle portico. The GPO had closed at three o'clock.

The gloaming air was cool and damp with the smell of the Liffey. Passers-by barely noticed, and saw nothing incongruous about, the traveler standing befront the post office. Holmes was in deep thought mode, standing with his right-hand resting on a pillar; trying, perhaps, to take the temperature of the city. Thoughts of the biblical account of the blinded Sampson, who, standing between the pillars of the temple, managed to bring down the church with his colossal strength. Holmes wondered if he, himself, was clever enough to save this city, Dublin, from self-destructing. For there was trouble in the dank air of this capital city, and it was via a 'sixth sense' that these vibrations of impending calamity were being fathomed and perceived.

Dublin, the 'fair city' in song, was creaking beneath the cadence of determined men drilling on parade. Bands of armed men had been marching through its streets, preparing. England at war was weaker, and the time for a 'Rising' was anon. Eftsoon, a cohort of patriots and poets would rise up from the chains and shackles of seven centuries to smite a deadly blow for Ireland. The pococurante Sassenach and his rapacious empire were soon to know the wrath of a handful of avenging angels, and the probity of a fistful of fearless men.

Holmes spent Holy Saturday evening roaming the streets of downtown Dublin in his disguise. Stopping in working-class pubs; the warm hospitality shown to his shabby, traveler identity was no surprise. The name, 'Oscklehr Moshel', amused the local boyos; elevating the silent, somber mood that seemed to have descended upon the city, itself. Becoming a foil for the lighthearted banter awakened by the name and persona of one, Oscklehr Moshel, afforded Holmes access to the inner circles of pub life on a Saturday night. Snippets of comments, glances, and gestures became evidence in the flawless mind of Holmes, of some portentous event to take place on Easter Sunday; not only in Dublin, but down the country! After spending an hour in each of five pubs in turn, Holmes knew it could only be a "Rising".

Dr. and Mrs. John H. Watson had been looking forward to a quiet, tranquil Easter Sunday, beyond the ken of 221-B Baker Street. They were relaxing on the veranda enjoying the view of their flowering garden, savoring and sharing a pot of tea after breakfast, when the telegram from Mrs. Hudson was delivered.

"But John, we had such a lovely day planned," said Mrs. Watson, "must you leave so soon?"

"Yes, dear. No telling what Holmes is involved in. Perhaps a predicament of some sort. It could very well be a matter of life and death. One can never know with Sherlock Holmes. I recall an incident when …"

"Forgive me, dear," she interrupted, "you are absolutely correct. After all, Holmes may be in danger!"

Holmes rose early on Easter Sunday, put a scone in his pocket, and set out to locate the point of the Rising – the forming up location. He had concluded it would be at Liberty

Hall; presuming that historical symbolism would dictate that the 'Final Rising' for liberty can only begin at a hall named in its honor.

He began walking south on Sackville. He passed the Parnell Monument and continued on toward downtown. Just beyond the Imperial Hotel, which was across from the GPO, he stopped at a newsstand for a paper. The Sunday Independent had a column by one, Eoin MacNeill, calling off the military maneuvers which had been scheduled to take place this very day. MacNeill was the head of the Irish Volunteers. Holmes was nonplussed and feeling disappointed. For if truth be known, he was inclined towards having the Rising!

Editor's Note:

The astute reader will wonder how this narrator came to know of the deepest thoughts and emotions of Sherlock Holmes during the period of the 1916 Rising. As in other stories in this volume, a form of retrospective, clairvoyant telepathy was involved.

End Note.

Holmes walked on. At Abbey Street he turned left and went as far as Beresford Place to find Liberty Hall. He observed activity outside the hall as a crowd of men in uniform and carrying rifles was milling about. A smaller group, of women, in another type of uniform, was also present. A bookstore across the street caught Holmes' eye. He went and sat on its entrance step and pretended to be reading his newspaper. A member of the Volunteers came across the street to inquire about the intentions of the foreign vagabond.

Moshel stood up and opened his frock coat to reveal an inside lining with pockets filled with candy sticks: licorice and peppermint. Delighted, the militiaman escorted the peddler across the street to meet his comrades-in-arms. Moshel the candy man became known to the Dublin Militia.

Watson had spent a quiet Sunday afternoon reading in his easy chair at the Baker Street flat. At times he forgot that Holmes was in Dublin and not somewhere in the rooms with him. Mrs. Hudson brought up the tea and sandwiches an hour early, at three o'clock, in order to attend an open-air lecture in Hyde Park, by one of the more well-known 'soapbox speakers'. The Ukranian layabout was to meet her there. Afterwards, another 'pysanky' session was planned, at his digs. A wee fire of sweet-smelling peat expelled the dampness of a soft rain shower and lulled Watson into dream land.

The telephone downstairs in the vestibule began ringing at five o'clock. Watson awoke and hurried down to answer it.

"Dr. Watson here."

"Were you enjoying your nap, Watson?"

"Holmes! Where are you? How did you know I was napping?"

"Rudimentary, my dear fellow. You answered on the eleventh ring. Before I left, I timed a practice run from my chair to the telephone downstairs. Seven rings is ample time to descend the stairs to answer it."

"Pish and pshaw, Holmes; to you and the horse you rode in on."

"Jocosity becomes you, Watson. The Irish would find our verbal shenanigans bloody marvelous. However, I must revert to my signature demeanor, in light of the imminent rebellion here in Ireland; although the traditional and preferred term is a 'Rising'."

"I was upstairs reading one of your books on the history of Ireland ,when you rang up; actually, as you deduced, I had slipped into dozing. I hadn't known the frequency of the Irish Risings; nearly every generation has one. What with England at war in Europe, the Irish are bound to try one more."

"Precisely, Watson. There was a Rising planned for today, Easter Sunday; I am certain of it. But it was called off at the last moment. I do not know why. Nor do I know if it has been re-scheduled."

"Shall I inform Scotland Yard ... or the Prime Minister?"

"Were this any other country involved, I would not hesitate to do so, Watson; although no hard evidence has surfaced. But this is Ireland, the object of half of my ancestral fealty, rising up against the other half. If truth be known, after seven hundred years of English domination, my emotional sympathies are with the Irish people. Nevertheles, the idea of hostilities between the two countries is repugnant to me and I will do everything possible to avert such a calamity."

"Indeed! I am almost speechless, Holmes. With one foot in England and the other foot in Ireland, are you planning to walk the knife-edge of treason?"

"Are you sitting down, dear Watson? For I have a bombshell to drop on you. When you are a citizen of both countries, as I am and have been for many years, your allegiance must be a full fifty percent to each, in peace and in war, to avoid giving the impression, however miniscule, of favoritism."

"But Holmes, I know you! You are British, truly."

"Yes, Watson, I am. But I am also Irish! And, while you hold the dominant cultural bias of the typical Englishman against the Irish, based in large part on the alleged superiority of the conquering nation; I am predisposed to harbor an opposite prejudice; the worldwide archetype ingrained in all peoples, which instinctively sides with the victim and against the bully."

"It's flabbergasted I am, Holmes. This beats all."

"Calm yourself, my friend. Do not let the foudroyant nature of this conversation upset your equilibrium. My royal brandy is in the decanter under the big dictionary, on the lower shelf. Pour yourself a snifter when you go to look up 'foudroyant'."

"If you insist."

"Above all else, remain in the premises around the clock. A powderkeg of emotions has been assembled here in Dublin and its auspicious detonation may be inevitable. Good night and God Bless!"

The lanes end byways of Dublin town were electrified with the passing of dynamic men bulging with chargeable secrets. Each man impacted by the other in passing; like particles in motion, whose eventual coming together would generate a cataclysm.

One neutral man moved about them easily, immune to the collective tenseness; the candy man, recently adopted as the mascot of the Dublin Brigade.

Oscklehr Moshel once again made the rounds of some local pubs in Dublin. Whereas the previous night he had been north of the Liffey, in the area between Monto and the lower end of Sackville Street; this night he crossed over the Halfpenny Bridge and conducted a one-man pub crawl in the locale bounded by Trinity College, St. Stephen's Green, and Dublin Castle.

The pubs, though open, were quiet this night of Easter Sunday. A trickle of light-hearted tourists deviated from the somber ambience that had descended upon the publiners this hush-hush night. Holmes had anticipated a different pub scenario from the race of people known for their 'Irish wakes" lasting three days and nights. The risen Christ should be, and normally was, celebrated for the miracle of his rising from the grave. The Irish people have been rising, once each generation, for hundreds of years, struggling to unchain themselves from a bondage imposed on them by their English congeners.

At a small pub named O'Gorman's, in Drury Street, a militiaman stood the final round for Moshel the candyman, who in the eyes of the customer was a live Pasquinade for the itinerant jew peddler. The pub owner, Tomas O'Gorman, had begun to regale Moshel with the tales of the west of Ireland and County Clare.

"The women of Ireland are praying the rosary this night, as we stand here drinking our last pints, with a fervor seen but once in a lifetime," soliloquized the barman as he deposited the final shilling of the evening into the cigar box behind the bar.

The nightly closing of a pub in Ireland must set the saints themselves to laughing. On this occasion, as O'Gorman wrestled the few other guests out the front door, the militiaman had a friendly grip on the left arm of Moshel, preventing his lawful departure.

With the exodus onto the street accomplished, O'Gorman pulled a closing round of pints and came out from behind the bar to take a seat with customers permitted to finish their 'closing pint' after the closing hour. Then, remembering the last lookabout for stragglers, he drug a sleeping boyo from under the last booth and put him out in the rear alley.

During this 'last pint drinking', Moshel was mostly silent, but smiling, as this Dublin duo performed for the country man: the tall tales of O'Gorman being told in the foreground; while the sad songs of Ireland were being sung in the background, by the militiamen.

They were all captured in the wimple of time that is only to be found in the Celtic lands of these Isles of Britain; in the Gaelic slue that meanders through these local pubs, where the current of humanity washes away the frippery of its false colors and the fantasy of its gasconade; in a slice of time experienced nowhere else.

The 'last pint drinking' time in Ireland, the interval between the legal closing time and the moment when the last man out departs the pub, varies with the weather and the fortunes of the local sports team. But the Irish pub owners, a breed apart and known for their pragmatism and shrewdness, have mostly agreed to instruct their barmen to make it out of the pub before the crack of dawn each morning.

And so, twas a wee bit past three in the morning of Easter Monday, when three blighters lept out of O'Gorman's Pub into a miasmal mist and headed for the bridge over the river Liffey; two insisting Irishmen escorting one reluctant recusant. At the HalfPenny Bridge the prisoner of hospitality feigned an impending stomach upheaval, by which he broke free and scampered across the narrow footbridge and vanished into the fog.

"Slan abhaile!" the escorts called out to their disappearing charge.

By eleven o'clock in the morning, Holmes, as Moshel, had returned to the vicinity of Drury Street. He had gleaned some references to 'the boys will be showing up at Liberty Hall by noon tomorrow', while he was sleuthing in the pubs last night. Columns of armed men were coming and going; shouldering rifles, muskets, shovels, pitchforks, and Irish war clubs; some had uniforms, some did not. Some were not armed.

With all the commotion, Holmes made his way to the bookstore unnoticed by those he encountered yesterday. Once inside, he sat in a chair in the reading area by the storefront window. While pretending to peruse a book, he was able to observe the situation out in the street. He read between the lines of the comings and goings, arrivals and departures, of companies of militiamen; deciphering a deployment plan out of what would seem mass confusion to lessor mortals.

A cadre of leaders was in command, and they were disbursing their troops to various locations throughout the town. An unrecognized flag was flying over Liberty Hall. It was a tricolor of green, white, and orange. The uniforms of the Irish Volunteers were in various shades of green, mostly.

So caught up in the moment was Holmes, that he failed to notice the scrutiny he was under. The bookmonger had him in his sights, metaphorically speaking, ever since Holmes began staring over top of the book he was holding and out the bay window.

By noon the remaining assemblage had been formed up in a marching column about one hundred and fifty strong. At noon, three leaders led them away in military fashion. A column of seven score men, one woman, and a follower twenty yards behind, bringing up the rear; the itinerant, vagabond mascot.

A march into the forever annals of human history; one to be remembered unto the endtimes; a handful of poets and dreamers were leading a company of Irish Volunteers into battle against the British Empire!

There was one woman in the advancing column. A throwback to the remarkable fighting women in Celtic history and legend; one intrepid female warrior, peerless and incomparable, *sui generis,* to become the first of her gender to stand upon the free ground of the embryonic Republic of Ireland!

At Sackville Street, upon command, the column did a competent 'column right' and dominated the way northwards, shunting lesser traffic aside. The crowd of holiday shoppers took little or no notice of what they assumed was just another practice drill of the wooden-rifle militia.

Befront the General Post Office the column was halted.

Dr. John Watson had abandoned the company of his comely wife, with some reluctance. Her effervescent personality had become the joy of his agedness; her light-heartedness the counterbalance to the pensiveness of Holmes.

When the telephone rang at noon, Watson was standing on the front steps, enjoying some fresh air after a rain shower. He stepped inside the partly open entrance door, latched it, and opened the inner vestibule door, to reach the telephone on the foyer wall, opposite the pocket doors to Mrs. Hudson's parlor.

"Hello! Dr. Watson here."

"Hello John, Sherlock here. Listen carefully, and for the love of God, don't interrupt!"

"O.K., Holmes," said Watson, interrupting.

"I'm in Dublin, befront the General Post Office, which is under attack by Irish militiamen. Shots have been fired. The Irish have sent scores of troops to seal off both ends of Sackville Street while another four score have seized the post office. There are additional troops in position around the city. It's a Rising! The Irish are Rising again!

"I'm in a public telephone booth out front, at the south end of the portico, partially concealed from view. I'm going inside the building to try and prevent any more shooting. I'll call when I can. Do not reveal my whereabouts. Stay near the telephone. Goodbye."

Watson was stunned by Holmes' report. A premonition of peril came upon him concerning his partner in crime detection. He felt duty-bound to inform the English government at once, despite the risk to Holmes' reputation, so he immediately had the telephone company operator connect him to the residence of the Prime Minister.

"Hello! This is Dr. John Watson, of Sherlock Holmes and Watson, calling the Prime Minister on a most urgent matter."

"The Prime Minister is in a luncheon meeting. Can I take a message?"

"Yes, by all means. Kindly tell him that the Irish are rising in Dublin!"

Several English soldiers were taken prisoner inside the GPO as they were conducting personal business at the counters. The Irish customers were released, along with the postal clerks. Gunfire was heard coming from both ends of Sackville Street. Moshel went into the post office as the civilians were coming out.

One lone English officer suddenly appeared, as if from nowhere, and rushed toward the leaders of the assault, who were occupying the center of the great hall. Just as rapidly, he was tackled and brought down hard on the marble floor by a spry older man in country attire. They wrestled and a shot was fired by the downed officer before several rebels were able to subdue him and lead him away. The tackler lay mortally wounded.

"This man saved your life, Mr. Pearse!" said a militiaman who was kneeling beside the wounded man. "That English officer was heading straight for you and would have shot you down dead!"

The quiet leader, called Pearse, made the sign of the cross before speaking: "Send for one of our nurses. We must save this stranger. Does anyone know who he is?"

"I do!," sang out a voice from the stairs leading up to the upper storey, "he's the gypsy peddler from Liberty Hall, the one the boys picked to be the mascot of the Irish Volunteers." The big man, speaking, then ran up to secure the second floor.

Once the building was secured and some prisoners had been taken, the leader, Pearse, came outside, to stand under the new flag of the Irish Republic, and to read aloud the Proclamation of The Provisional Government; by which "… in the name of God and of the dead generations …' the current and future generations would mark this day forever.

Members of the women's organization, *Cumann na mBan,* including several Red Cross nurses, reported to the GPO for duty; to set up a meals kitchen and an infirmary. The vagabond with the chest wound received special attention as 'the man what saved Pearse". All the subsequent wounded, including English soldiers, were treated impartially.

By day's end, members of the newly named Irish Republican Army were in possession of key locations around the city, after skirmishes with British troops. Sherlock Holmes, in disguise as Oscklehr Moshel, had been attended by a surgeon and was recuperating in a safe location; while under the care of a Red Cross nurse.

Editor's Note:

Five days into the Republic, on 29 May, the head of the Provisional Government, P. H. Pearse, signed an unconditional surrender statement; ordering his forces throughout Ireland to give up the fight.

Five days later, on 3 May, in the early morning darkness of English justice, Pearse was summarily executed behind the walls of Kilmainham Jail!

They shot Tom Clark next! And Thomas MacDonagh after him!

They shot Joe Plunkett at dawn on 4 May! Then they led out Edward Daly and shot him! Next they brought out Michael O'Hanrahan, and shot him! Lastly that morning, out came Willie Pearse, eager to join his brother, and they shot him!

On 5 May, they shot Major John MacBride!

On 8 May, they shot Eamonn Ceannt! And they shot Michael Mallin! And they shot Sean Heuston! And they shot Con Colbert!

On 12 May, they shot Sean MacDermott! Then they brought out James Connolly, too weak to stand, sat him in a chair by the wall of execution, and they shot him!

The remaining 97 condemned to die for taking part in the rebellion had there sentences commuted to prison time, by the English Prime Minister, Asquith; after an outcry of outrage from around the world!

End Note.

After two weeks of complete bedrest, his Irish angel had her hero of the rising, Oscklehr Moshel, up and about her wee cottage down the country. She was still being hunted by the British for participating in the rebellion – as they called it. He had been resting here since the first day of the Rising; she came to relieve the earlier nurse on the last day of the Rising, after almost being nabbed by a squad of Brits. Her name was Winifred Carney, and she was the sole female in the initial assault on the British Empire.

"It's time we got you out of the country," she said to her patient. "Have you somewhere to go?"

"I do," he said, smiling.

"And would you be telling me?" she asked, feigning umbrage.

"I'll return from whence I came, across the Irish Sea."

"O.K., so. But you'll have to stand on your own two feet. A man in a wheelchair will be stopped at the ferry and taken in for questioning, for sure. We'll send a man along with you as far as you need him, to hold onto."

"I'll be fine alone, once I have a seat on the train to London, leaving from Holyhead in Wales. I have a friend in London who will look after me."

Holmes was pale and weary when he arrived in London on the train from Holyhead. The conductor was helping him from the train when I took my friend into my charge. By his pallor and shallow breathing, I knew he had been seriously injured. He told me little, since it hurt him to speak at length.

I whistled for a Clarence cab, so Holmes could lie down during the ride home to Baker Street. Mrs. Hudson and I helped him up the stairs and into his bed. "With Mrs. Hudson's cooking and my medical skills," I thought to myself, "he'll be right as rain in a fortnight."

As I handed Mrs. Hudson the vagabond clothing he had arrived home wearing – to be scalded clean of bloodstains and donated to the poor – she noticed a folded note in the inside pocket of the cloak. I took it from her without a word said, so anxious was I to learn something of Holmes' venture during the three weeks he was gone.

The unfolded note read as follows:

---

15 June 1916

A Dhuine Uasal

By saving Pearse's life in the first minutes of the assault on the GPO, you enabled the Rising to unfold and to reach its climax.

Once again the Brits have given us our "Fenian dead". The seventeen executed martyrs, may God Bless them all, will depress the scales of human compassion deep enough to incite the forces that will free this holy island, once and for all time.

Your name (unspoken herein to protect you should this letter fall into evil hands) shall be whispered down the future generations of free Irish, men and women; the man who saved Padraic Pearse in the Rising of 1916.

Aithnionn ciarog ciarog eile.

The Big Fella

The Secret Adventures of Sherlock Holmes

by **Paul E. Heusinger**

I.S.B.N. 1-59879-153-2

Order Online at:
www.authorstobelievein.com

By Phone Toll Free at:
1-877-843-1007